AN UNLIKELY SEDUCTION

ELIZABETH KELLY

EK PUBLISHING INC.

Published by
EK Publishing Inc.

ISBN-13: 978-1-988826-05-9

Cover art by
EK Designs

AN UNLIKELY SEDUCTION

Who will win this game of seduction?

Two years after the tragic death of his wife, Caleb Thornwell lives a solitary life. When he rescues a fragile and innocent woman named Ellie from a blizzard, he's surprised by his attraction to her. His discovery that Ellie is the daughter of the man who killed his wife sets a plan of revenge into motion.

Seducing Ellie into giving him her innocence is easy, but he isn't prepared for his reaction to her soft touch or his sudden desire to protect her.

Ellie Walters didn't plan on running off in a blizzard. But she's left with no choice when the man her father is demanding she marry tries to violate her. Certain she's going to die in the blizzard, she's shocked when she wakes up in a strange man's bed.

That's embarrassing enough, but her immediate and heated response to his rough hands and whispered demands is downright shameful. Trapped in Caleb's home until the blizzard ends, she concocts a plan of seduction to avoid a marriage she doesn't want.

Seducing Caleb into taking her innocence is easy, but protecting her heart may prove too difficult.

Please Note: An Unlikely Seduction is a western historical romance novella. It's hotter than your usual Elizabeth Kelly books, so proceed with caution and a clean pair of panties. Expect scorching sex scenes and a dirty-talking hero who isn't shy about what he wants in bed.

* * *

CHAPTER 1

S he was going to die.

The snowstorm had turned into a blizzard, and she'd been stumbling through the howling wind and blowing snow for what felt like hours. Despite her gloves and boots, her feet and hands were completely numb, and her eyes stung from the hard pellets of ice and snow.

She shouldn't have run away. She should have brained the violating bastard with the rock again until he stopped moving. But she was afraid - terrified, actually. Frederick had already been staggering to his feet with blood pouring from his temple. The look of rage on his face had wiped away her anger and changed it to terror instantly. She had turned and fled.

She thought longingly of her horse, but Frederick stood between her and the horses. She knew without a doubt that any attempt to get to her horse would have resulted in her capture. Besides, she was positive that she was heading toward town even in her fear-induced race through the trees. An hour or two of walking and she would be safe in her own house. Once her father discovered what Frederick had tried to do, she would never again suffer through an evening of courtship with him.

As the snow began to fall more heavily and the temperature dropped, she was forced to admit she was lost. The knowledge sent another strong surge of adrenaline through her, but by the time she wandered to the forest's edge, that adrenaline was long gone. Knowing she was dead if she stopped, she trudged wearily on through the darkness with her head bowed against the wind and blinding snow. Her legs were weary from struggling through the knee-deep snow.

She was so tired. Had she ever been this tired in her life? She didn't think so. Each step required great effort and concentration, and it was starting to feel like too much work. What she wanted to do was to curl up in the snow and sleep. Yes, sleep was exactly what she needed. She would rest for a while. She would catch her breath, maybe take a short nap, and then continue.

Ellie, no! If you stop moving, you'll die!

She was dead anyway. Her body already knew it. Just because her brain took longer to accept it didn't make it any less true. She was going to die because she refused to let Frederick Barns take her virtue.

For one moment, she bitterly wished that she had just let him take what he wanted. Keeping her innocence seemed so important at the time. Despite what her father said and wanted, she wasn't entirely certain she wanted to be married to Frederick. If she allowed him to take her virginity, she would be left with no choice but to marry him.

The wind whipped at her skirt, lifting it around her knees as the snow seeped into her petticoats, making them grow heavier by the moment. When, at last, she stumbled and fell, she rested her head on her arms and closed her eyes. Sleep was what she wanted, what she needed.

* * *

"Easy. Easy, boy," Caleb murmured to the nervous horse. Outside the stable, the wind howled and moaned, and he patted the horse on his flank before moving to the next stall. The dairy cow wasn't bothered by the sound of the wind. She chewed contentedly at the hay, and he added more to her stall before latching it firmly. The blizzard was one of the worst he'd seen in the five years he'd been out west, and he stared down at the dog hovering near his feet.

"Ready to go back to the warm house, Scout?"

The dog panted happily. Caleb patted its flank affectionately as they moved to the barn door. He opened the heavy door and winced as the icy pellets of snow hit his face before he staggered out into the wind. He held the rope he had tied earlier from the house to the barn as Scout sniffed the air. The dog barked loudly and bounded from the path to the house.

"Scout, here!" he shouted. The wind took his voice and carried it away. He scowled before trudging a few feet after the dog. If the damn dog didn't come back, it would freeze to death. Hell, he'd freeze to death if he was foolish enough to chase after him. The house was invisible in the dark and the snow, and the barn was a rapidly diminishing dark shape. Only fools went after their dogs in a damn blizzard.

"Scout!" He shouted again and was rewarded by a loud whine.

Caleb stumbled forward a few feet. He cursed under his breath when his foot hit something solid and unmoving, and he pitched forward into the deep snow.

"What the hell?"

Scout was standing over the body of a woman. Already, the snow had drifted over her to cover a good portion of her body. He guessed that she had been lying on the ground for at least fifteen minutes, considering how much snow had already accumulated on her.

Where the hell had she come from, he wondered. Scout whined again before pawing anxiously at the woman's snow-covered hip. Caleb staggered to his feet and heaved the woman over his shoulder.

"Scout, come."

The dog and the man struggled through the deep snow to the rope visible in the blowing snow. Holding it tightly, Caleb bent his head against the wind and followed it to the house. Inside the warmth of the house, he set the woman on the sofa before shrugging out of his jacket and kicking off his boots. He stripped off his scarf and gloves as Scout licked the woman's pale face.

"Scout, get back." He gently pushed the dog away before unbuttoning the woman's jacket and pushing his hand under her scarf. Her skin was ice cold, and he grunted in surprise when he felt the faint but steady pulse in her neck.

"She's alive," he said to the dog. "But she won't be for long if I don't warm her up."

Moving quickly, he removed her outerwear and tugged off her boots. Her dress was made of fine silk. It was obvious she was no farmer's wife. He inhaled sharply when he unwound the scarf from around her face. She was beautiful. Her long dark hair was pinned to her scalp in a braid. Her dark lashes were long and thick, and she had a full mouth and high cheekbones. She was younger than him. Probably by at least five years, although he had never been good at guessing a woman's age.

He studied her carefully. She looked familiar to him, and he wondered if he had seen her on one of his infrequent trips to town. Not that she would have noticed him. A woman like her paid no attention to a man like him. She wore no ring on her left hand, and he frowned. What was a single woman doing out alone in the middle of a blizzard? His farm was nowhere close to town.

Does it matter, Caleb? She's going to die if you don't warm her up. Hell, she might die anyway.

Good point. He needed to warm her up quickly and check her feet for frostbite. He hesitated only briefly before removing her skirt and petticoats. She wore a corset but no bustle, and he wondered if she had been out riding. Of course, Missy had refused to wear a bustle even to town. Perhaps this woman was like her. He snorted out loud. She was nothing like Missy. Her hands were soft and smooth, and it was obvious that she had never worked a day of manual labour.

He unclipped her stockings and rolled them down her legs. Her skin was milky white, and he doubted it had ever seen a second of the sun. He checked her feet anxiously for frostbite. They were cold but not frozen, and he rubbed them briefly until they turned pink. He unbuttoned her bodice and removed it, ignoring the way his cock stirred at the sight of the woman's full breasts pushed into high mounds by the corset. He rolled her to her side to unlace her corset. God, he hated these things. Missy had worn them only when they went to town and then spent the entire time grumbling about her inability to breathe.

A smile crossed his lips. Missy had been unconventional when it came to fashion, he supposed. Hell, she'd been unconventional in many ways, and he loved her for it. Her fiery spirit and refusal to follow proper protocol attracted him from the start. When the last of her corsets had broken, she couldn't hide the look of glee from her face. He thought it was probably the one time she was thankful they were poor. He had preferred her without one anyway. He liked pulling a woman into his embrace and feeling her actual body, not layers of clothing and bone.

He pulled the corset from the woman's body and dropped it to the floor before rolling her onto her back. The woman took what he was confident was her first deep breath of the day and muttered softly. He leaned over her and cupped her cold face.

"Miss? Miss, can you hear me? Open your eyes."

Her eyelids fluttered open, and she stared blearily at him. Her eyes were the colour of warm amber, and he stared in fascination at them.

"Cold," she whispered. "So cold."

Her body was beginning to shiver. He considered the shivering a good sign and patted her shoulder through the thin chemise she wore. "You'll be warmer soon. What's your name?"

"Ellie," she sighed before closing her eyes.

He hesitated again before removing her drawers. The bottom half of them was soaked through, as was the bottom of her chemise, but he decided against stripping her completely naked. If the chemise stopped her from warming up, he would remove it later. For now, he would use blankets and body heat to try and warm her.

Leaving her wet clothes on the floor, he lifted her into his arms again. She was much lighter without the mountain of clothing, and he frowned a little at how fragile and slender she seemed. She was a much more delicate woman than he was used to, and he needed to be gentle with her.

Gentle? What exactly are you planning on doing to the woman?

He ignored his inner voice and carried her into the bedroom. He tucked her into the bed before stripping off all his clothes except his drawers. He slid into the bed beside her and piled the blankets and quilts over them. He tugged her into his embrace. To his surprise, she immediately put her arms around him and flattened her shivering body against his.

"Warm," she whispered before burying her face in his neck.

He held her tightly and rubbed her cold skin through her chemise. He pushed experimentally at her smooth thighs with his rough one and made a low grunt of surprise when she parted them immediately. He pushed his thigh up snugly against her naked crotch. It was the only part of her that was even remotely warm. He rubbed her cold leg. Perhaps she was not as innocent as she appeared.

Or maybe she's just really cold.

Maybe. He pulled the woman even closer and closed his eyes.

CHAPTER 2

S he was so warm. Was she in hell? Had she died in the blizzard and been sent to hell for her sins?

Sins? What sins? You're a good girl.

Was she? Did a good girl go on an unchaperoned horse ride with a man?

Your father insisted, remember? He said Frederick was so well-respected that your reputation would remain intact.

She tried to move, a thin thread of panic welling inside of her when she realized she was trapped. Something thick and heavy pressed against her waist, and she forced her eyes open. Her eyes widened immediately. She was pressed up intimately against a stranger. A stranger with dark hair, a long beard, a crooked nose, and – good God – what exactly was that hardness pressing against her hip?

She tried to move away, her breath coming in harsh pants as adrenaline pulsed through her veins. She made a frightened squeak when the stranger's arm tightened around her waist, and he frowned in his sleep.

"Sir?" She whispered. "Sir, please wake up."

His eyelids fluttered. He had ridiculously long lashes for a man, and she inhaled sharply when he stared sleepily at her. His eyes were incredibly blue, as blue as the ocean she missed so terribly. She stared wide-eyed at him as he smiled hazily, and his big hand moved from her waist to cup the back of her head.

He pressed his mouth against hers, his beard tickling her lips as his tongue probed at the seam of her lips. She parted them automatically and gasped when he slid his tongue into her mouth with a sensual flicking motion that made heat bloom in her belly.

Her nipples tightened, and her pelvis began to ache as he pressed her onto her back and flung one heavy thigh across hers. His hand slipped under the loose neckline of her chemise and cupped her breast with shocking intimacy. He growled his approval at her pebbled nipple and pinched it lightly before kissing her more deeply.

She moaned, and her back arched involuntarily. She had kissed a man before, Frederick, in fact. But they were chaste kisses in her home's parlour while her father sat in the next room, reading his newspaper. She had never allowed Frederick to put his tongue in her mouth or let his hands wander anywhere but her arms and shoulders, but the touch of his mouth had never affected her like this.

The stranger's kisses were wonderful despite the ticklish nature of his beard. The feel of his rough fingers against her sensitive nipple made shivers run up and down her spine. Frederick had hands nearly as soft as her own. She had no idea that a hand, rough from hard labour, could feel so good against her skin.

He pulled on her nipple. It was beginning to throb in a way that was both pleasurable and a little painful. She moaned again when he kissed down her neck and licked at her collarbone.

"Oh, oh, please," she whispered.

She wasn't entirely certain what she was begging for, but the stranger seemed to know. He tugged her chemise down until her breasts were bared. Embarrassment immediately flooded through her. When she tried to preserve her modesty by tugging the material back into place, that rough hand grabbed her wrists and stretched her arms above her head as he pushed his thigh between hers.

"No," he growled. "I want to see them. Taste them."

She frowned. What did he mean he wanted to taste them? Her silent question was answered when he bent his head and latched onto her nipple, sucking heavily at it.

"Oh!" The little squeak of pleasure had escaped before she could stop it, and she writhed against him as he teased her nipple into an erect peak. He switched to her other breast, teasing and licking at the nipple until it was as stiff as the first one. His fingers pulled at her right nipple as his lips pulled at the left one, and she realized that the little whines and moans of pleasure she could hear were coming from her.

"Please," she moaned. She should have been ashamed at the obvious need she could hear in her voice. She should have been embarrassed at the way she was humping his leg.

"Do you like that?" he muttered, and she nodded eagerly.

"Yes, please don't stop."

He raised his head and stared at her. An odd look was coming over his face, one that suggested he was realizing this wasn't a dream. She pressed her mouth against his frantically. She didn't think she was very good at kissing, but she pushed timidly at his lips with her tongue anyway. To her delight, he opened his mouth, and she licked tentatively at the inside of his mouth. He groaned, and her pelvis throbbed when he sucked on her tongue.

Oh, this was wonderful. She could lie in this bed and kiss the stranger forever. He released her hands, and she moved them tentatively to his chest. Hair covered it, and she touched the wiry strands gently. When her fingers grazed over one flat nipple, he jerked and moaned against her mouth. Still kissing him, she ran her fingers across his nipple again. Were they as sensitive as hers, she wondered. Would it drive him just as crazy if she sucked on them? She pinched it experimentally, and he growled softly before nipping at her bottom lip.

"Little minx," he whispered and pinched her nipple in return.

She twitched against him and moved her hands across his flat abdomen before tracing his broad back. He was delightfully warm, and she touched the large muscles before moving lower. He was wearing underclothes, and she wasn't sure if that was a tingle of disappointment or relief she was feeling.

"I can feel how wet your little pussy is," he suddenly whispered into her ear, and her face flamed bright red. For the first time, she realized that while he might be wearing underclothes, she wasn't. She could feel his hair-roughened thigh rubbing directly against her warmth.

She struggled to get away from him, and he shook his head before reaching down and cupping her between her legs. Her eyes widened when his fingers brushed against an extremely sensitive spot.

"Oh my God!" she cried, and he grinned before kissing her firmly.

"Like that, do you? Your little pearl is very wet and swollen," he said. He rubbed again, and her entire body arched off the bed as pleasure, so strong it made her lose her breath, rushed through her.

"What – what is that?" she moaned.

He stiffened against her, his fingers slowing to a stop. He ignored her when she made a whine of protest and dug her nails into his broad back.

"Please, I want more," she begged shamelessly.

He was frowning, and she stared wide-eyed at him when his finger breached her tight entrance. She winced and tried to close her legs. His fingers rubbing against her felt good – felt amazing, actually – but that certainly didn't.

"Please touch me again," she whispered.

"Bloody hell," he muttered.

She blinked in confusion when he yanked his hand out from between her legs and threw the covers back. He sat up, swung his legs out of bed and sat on the edge of it.

"Sir?" Her face flaming with embarrassment, she tugged her chemise over her still-throbbing breasts and sat up. She scooted away until her back rested against the wall and made a soft moan of dismay.

What had she done? She didn't even know this man's name, and she had kissed him, allowed him to touch her intimately and enjoyed it. Craved it. Her entire body cried out for release from the tension coiling in her pelvis. She clamped her legs together in an effort to ease the odd ache between them. What was happening to her?

"You're a virgin," he said without turning to look at her.

"Yes, of course, I am," she whispered as her cheeks burned.

He craned his head to stare at her, and she shrank back at his look of dark lust. "You don't act like a virgin."

She wanted to die of embarrassment. If she could have sunk through the floorboards, she would have. Instead, she gathered the bedclothes and her tattered pride around her like a thick cloak and forced herself to meet his gaze.

"I am a proper lady, and you should be ashamed of touching me like you were."

He barked laughter before standing and reaching for his pants. "You weren't asking me to stop, lady. In fact, I'm pretty sure I heard you begging me for more."

His gaze dropped to her pelvis. "Your pussy definitely wanted more."

"How dare you," she whispered. "I won't allow you to speak to me in such a manner. You are coarse and rude and -"

He rolled his eyes as he buttoned his pants and yanked his shirt over his head. "Considering I saved you from freezing to death last night, I think you can forgive my lack of manners just this once."

Before she could reply, he had left the bedroom, shutting the door firmly behind him. She stayed where she was, blinking back the hot tears as a dog barked, and she heard the stranger's deep voice murmuring in reply. She rested her head on her knees and took a few deep breaths. She was out of the cold and perfectly fine, so why did she feel like she was in more trouble now than when she was lost in the blizzard?

* * *

BREAKFAST WAS ALMOST FINISHED COOKING WHEN SHE FINALLY emerged from the bedroom. Caleb watched as she patted Scout's head tentatively when he approached her. His tail wagged, and a faint smile crossed her face when he licked at her hands. She had wrapped the quilt from the bed around her body, and he frowned at the way the edge of it dragged across the dirty floor. Missy's mother had made the quilt for her. Missy had never quite mastered the art of sewing, and the quilt was precious to her. He realized the woman was staring at him, and her cheeks flushed before she lifted the quilt up so the ends wouldn't drag on the floor.

"I'm sorry."

He grunted in reply, and she hurried quickly across the small living room to where he had laid her clothing on the floor next to the fire this morning. They were still soaking wet, and a look of dismay crossed her face. He supposed he should have laid them out last night, but he was a bit preoccupied with saving her life.

"They're going to take a while to dry," he said.

The blizzard was still raging, and the small house was cold despite the fire. His home was well built, but when the weather dropped to this temperature, even the best built houses on the prairie were nearly impossible to keep warm. His was no exception.

He glanced at her bare feet. They had to be freezing, and he briefly considered offering her a pair of his socks before dismissing the idea. Best not to do anything nice for the woman. What had happened in the bedroom was a mistake. He should never have touched her that way and wouldn't have if he hadn't been dreaming of Missy. He had simply mistaken the woman for his dead wife, and why wouldn't he have? He hadn't taken a woman to his bed since she had died, so it was only natural his sleep-fogged brain thought she was Missy.

Bullshit. You might have been dreaming of Missy, but you knew it wasn't her the moment you opened your eyes.

He ignored his inner voice and placed the platter of eggs and pancakes on the table.

"Breakfast is ready," he grunted.

She stared nervously at him. "Oh, no thank you. I've imposed enough on you as it is. I'm not going to eat your food as well."

He scowled at her, and she smiled tentatively. "I'll eat once the blizzard ends, and I am at home. Besides, I am not hungry."

Her stomach growled loudly with perfect timing, and a dull pink coloured her cheeks.

"The blizzard won't end for a few days," he said. "Sit and eat."

"A few days?" she whispered. "Are you certain?"

He nodded and pulled out his chair before sitting and piling pancakes and eggs onto his plate.

My darling, this woman is your guest, and you're being rude. Wait for her to join you before eating.

Missy's voice spoke in his head, and he shoved it out immediately. He didn't want to think of Missy. He didn't want to hear her voice in his head only half an hour after he had touched another woman so intimately.

Please, it's been over two years since I died. Do you believe I expected you to remain celibate? I know better than anyone of your appetite for sex.

This time, Missy's voice spoke dryly in his head and he actually blushed a little.

I'm not spoiling your memory - our love - with a quick, meaningless roll in the hay, he argued.

Perhaps, my darling, that is exactly what you need.

The woman is a virgin. Once this blizzard ends, I'll never see her again. Do you want me to spoil her innocence that way?

Missy remained silent on the subject of spoiled innocence, and he sighed before gruffly saying, "You need to eat. There's plenty of food."

"If you are certain," she said softly.

He nodded, and she drifted closer, keeping the quilt around her as she sat in the chair across from his.

"Thank you," she said.

He grunted again in reply and shoveled the pancakes and eggs into his mouth. She took a single pancake and cut a small piece with her knife and fork. She chewed it delicately, and a strange look came over her face before she swallowed it with difficulty.

"It's very good."

He rolled his eyes. He had no abilities in the kitchen, and two years of cooking his own meals hadn't improved them.

She ate half of the pancake before setting down her fork and knife. He eyed her thin face. If that was all she ate, it was no wonder she was so slender and fragile. Missy had been short and sturdy with full curves that fit perfectly against him. This woman was tall with a willowy frame and looked like a strong wind would blow her over. Although he admitted grudgingly to himself, her breasts were amazing. Much fuller than her slender frame should have allowed for. And her nipples – the way they had swelled in his mouth, the way she had responded when he had pinched and pulled at them – just the memory of it was making his cock harden in his pants.

He snorted inwardly and scraped the rest of his plate clean. The woman was too fragile for him. If he were ever ready to find another wife, he would find someone more like Missy. Someone strong and able to contribute to the harsh life on the prairie. He needed another Missy, not the frightened little bird before him.

She survived a blizzard, did she not, my darling? Missy whispered in his head. *Stop comparing her to me. That isn't fair to the poor, sweet girl.*

"I wondered if we could start over?" The woman's soft voice interrupted his internal dialogue.

He stared at her, and she smiled timidly. "Perhaps we could forget about what happened earlier and start over?"

He nodded, and she held out her hand. "My name is Ellie. Ellie Walters."

His hand, which had automatically been reaching for hers, stopped. His entire body froze before he dropped his hand.

She gave him a cautious look. "Are you all right? You're very pale."

"Walters," he rasped. "Your father is the doctor in town?"

"Yes," she said. "Do you know him?"

17

He shook his head, and she licked her lips nervously as he stared at her. "I – you haven't told me your name."

"Caleb Thornwell." He watched her carefully, but there was no reaction to his name. Although he supposed her father wouldn't have given her details of the man whose wife and baby daughter he had murdered.

"It's nice to meet you, Mr. Thornwell," she said warmly. "Thank you for saving my life last night. I'm incredibly grateful."

He stood up abruptly, knocking his chair over. Her eyes widened in alarm.

"Mr. Thornwell? Did I say something wrong?"

He grabbed his jacket from the hook by the door. "I need to feed the animals. Don't leave the house."

He opened the door, letting the cold wind and snow swirl in, and whistled for Scout before slamming the door shut behind him.

* * *

CALEB STOOD AT THE BARN DOOR AS SCOUT STARED CURIOUSLY at him. He had finished the chores nearly fifteen minutes ago, and the dog was clearly wondering why they weren't headed to the house with the bucket of milk and the eggs he had gathered from the few hens he kept.

Anger was bubbling through his entire body, and he took several deep breaths. He had dreamed of revenge against the doctor for two years, and now he had the only child of his enemy in his house. He realized why she looked slightly familiar to him. He had met her once before. About a month after he and Missy had moved out west, they had gone to town for supplies. The doctor and his daughter were in the general store, and they spoke briefly. The girl had complimented Missy on her dress. She couldn't have been more than twenty at the time, and her wealthier status over theirs was apparent. Missy was impressed by her sweet and kind nature. So many of the wealthy looked down on the farmers and miners – the doctor was no exception to that with his obvious impatience to end their brief encounter - but she had spoken to Missy as her equal.

He rubbed his forehead. He had the doctor's daughter, but he had no idea what to do with her. How could he use her to take his revenge against her father for the loss of his beloved wife and their newborn daughter?

His eyes widened, and he stared blankly at the dog at his feet. Of course - it was perfect. The woman was not unattractive, and she certainly responded to his touch. He would take her innocence. Her father would be horrified to discover a poor farmer took his precious daughter's virginity. Money and privilege mattered to the man, and to know that his daughter had willingly given away her innocence to someone who possessed neither would drive him mad.

My darling, don't do this. The girl has done nothing to you and does not deserve such cruelty. Please, my darling, don't –

He shoved Missy's voice out of his head with an ease he would never have thought he was capable of before this moment. Ellie meant nothing to him. If she had to suffer for her father's sins, so be it. He had suffered daily for the last two years. What did he care if she suffered too?

* * *

ELLIE PACED IN THE SMALL HOUSE. THE KITCHEN AND LIVING room were one big room, and three smaller rooms led off from the living room. One was Mr. Thornwell's bedroom, the other appeared to be a second bedroom with a small daybed and dresser, and the third was completely empty except for a set of three locked trunks.

She studied the dirt on the floor before taking the broom that hung on the wall next to the door and sweeping. She had explored a bit. She used the chamber pot she found in the bedroom before emptying it out the back door and rinsing it clean. The quick exposure to the cold had taken her breath away. She washed and dried the few dishes from breakfast. She stood at the window for a while, studying the blowing snow that completely obliterated her ability to see further than a few feet. Her saviour had been gone for over an hour now. She considered putting her boots on and following the rope to the barn, but he had specifically told her to stay in the house.

She sighed and finished sweeping before hanging the broom neatly on its hook. She checked her clothing, but most of it was still rather wet. She picked up the quilt she had draped over the sofa and wrapped it around her body. She felt terribly exposed in her thin chemise and hoped her clothing would dry soon. She moved to the bookshelf tucked against the far wall and studied the books that lined its shelves. She loved to read, and she pulled a book from the shelf. If Mr. Thornwell didn't return in the next half hour, she would brave the weather and his anger and go to the barn.

The door opened, and he entered in a rush of cold air and snow. His dog, she thought he had called him Scout, shook the snow from his thick pelt. He barked softly at her before running over to her and prodding at her quilt-covered thigh with his cold nose.

"Hello, Scout," she said before scratching the thick fur around his neck. "Is that his name?"

Mr. Thornwell nodded as he placed the bucket of milk and a basket filled with a few eggs on the table. He removed his jacket and boots before lifting the cloth from the bucket of milk.

"The wind blew most of the milk out," he said. "It's one of the worst blizzards I've ever seen."

She smiled timidly at him. "The weather here in the west is certainly much more temperamental than in the east."

He smiled at her, revealing even white teeth, and her heartbeat sped up. She didn't find him particularly attractive with that wild and bushy beard, but he gave her a look that made warmth unfurl in her belly.

"It certainly is, Miss Walters," he said. "Have you been out west long?"

"Only six years or so," she said. "My father moved us out here after my mother died."

"I'm sorry to hear of the loss of your mother," he said gently.

She blinked in confusion. The gruff, scary man from breakfast had completely disappeared, and she was finding the new version of Caleb Thornwell to be completely disarming.

"Thank you, Mr. Thornwell. She was a wonderful woman, and I miss her very much."

It was true. Her father was not prone to displays of affection. Although she had no doubt of his love for her, she missed the affection and love from her mother on a daily basis – even six years later.

"Please, call me Caleb. We farmers aren't quite so formal," he said.

She smiled. "Then you must call me Ellie."

He studied the small kitchen before glancing at the floor. "Thank you for tidying the dishes and sweeping the floor."

"It was the least I could do," she said. "You saved my life, and I will be forever in your debt."

"Would you like some tea, Ellie?"

"I could make it," she said.

"No, please, you're my guest. Sit." He gestured to the table, and she sat down. He filled a kettle with water and placed it on the small woodstove.

"You have a lovely home, Mr. – Caleb," she said politely.

"Thank you. I'm sure it's not as large or extravagant as your home," he said.

"It's a bit smaller than my father's home," she admitted, "but I find it very nice."

He placed tea leaves in the teapot and poured boiling water into it before bringing it to the table with two mugs. As it steeped, he sat and studied her bare left hand.

"May I ask how old you are, Ellie?"

She cleared her throat. "I'm twenty-four."

She blushed slightly, wondering if Caleb would find it strange that she was unmarried. It was a little odd – she supposed it was why her father was pushing so hard for her to marry Frederick – but after what he had tried to do, she would risk remaining a spinster for a while longer.

"How old are you?" she asked curiously.

"I'm nearly thirty," he said.

"You live here alone?"

"My wife died two years ago."

She gave him a sympathetic look. "I'm very sorry, Caleb."

"Thank you," he said. "Why were you out in the blizzard?"

"I was out riding with - "

She hesitated as he poured the tea into their mugs.

"Riding with who?" he prompted.

"A man named Frederick Barns."

He blinked at her. "The banker?"

"Yes. Do you know him?"

"I know of him. Why were you riding with him?"

She took a sip of the steaming liquid. "We're courting, or rather, we were."

"Courting? He's at least forty, isn't he?"

She nodded. "Forty-five, actually, but my father is very

good friends with him and believes we would make a good match."

"Is that what you believe?" he asked bluntly.

She hesitated. "I did not think ill of Frederick, but I wasn't entirely certain I wished to marry him. However, my father says that at my age, I cannot afford to be picky about who I marry."

He scoffed loudly. "Twenty-four is hardly an old maid."

"In my father's eyes, it is," she replied.

"You're beautiful," he said, and she blushed furiously. "Surely, other younger men in town wanted to court you."

"There were a few," she admitted with embarrassment. "But my father did not approve of any of them the way he approved of Frederick. Anyway, Frederick asked me to go riding with him yesterday afternoon. I said no, my father was working and unavailable to act as a chaperone, but Frederick insisted that my father would approve of us being alone together. He was right. My father had no issues with it. He said that Frederick's reputation in town was such that being alone with him would cause no risk to my reputation."

She rubbed her finger across the rim of the mug. "We rode for a while, and Frederick suggested we dismount and take a short walk. It was already apparent there was a storm coming, and I wanted to return to my home, but he insisted. I thought he was going to ask for my hand in marriage."

"Did he?" Caleb asked quietly.

"No," she said before shifting uncomfortably in her chair. "We walked for longer than we should have. We had a small argument, I stormed off, and we were separated in the blizzard. I knew I needed to keep moving and thought I was walking toward town, but I was wrong."

She glanced at Caleb. He was frowning, and she was positive he saw right through her flimsy lie. It was confirmed when he leaned forward and said, "Tell me what actually happened."

She bit at her bottom lip and twitched nervously when Caleb's large hand covered her small one and squeezed gently before releasing. "Tell me the truth, Ellie."

"He started kissing me, started touching me in a very, uh, inappropriate manner. I told him no, but he wouldn't stop. He pinned me to the ground and was trying to," she swallowed thickly, "remove my clothing, and I hit him in the head with a rock."

She blinked rapidly to stave off the tears and gave him a nervous look. "I – I didn't kill him. There was a lot of blood, but he was on his feet, and he – he was very angry with me. I turned and ran. I shouldn't have run into a blizzard - I'm not usually such a foolish girl - but I was afraid," she finished in a whisper.

There was silence, and she risked a glance at the man sitting across from her. His tea sat forgotten in front of him, and an odd look of anger appeared on his face.

"It was my fault," she said quickly. "I should not have gone riding with Frederick alone, but I believed him trustworthy. He is, after all, a very good friend of my father's."

"It wasn't your fault, Ellie," Caleb said softly.

"He said such terrible things to me. He said that we would be married no matter what, and I might as well give him the prize between my legs now and get it over with. He said I was a silly little girl and the only thing of value about me was my virginity. He was almost obsessed with it."

She stared solemnly at Caleb. "Why is a woman's virginity so important to a man? Do you care if a woman is innocent when you take her to your bed?"

Before he could reply, she flushed deeply and dropped her gaze to the table. "I'm so sorry. It is impolite of me to ask such personal questions."

She traced her finger over the worn wood of the table. "When my father finds out what happened, he will be so angry with Frederick. He trusts him, and knowing what his friend has done will grieve him deeply. He will not approve of Frederick's courtship now."

There was no reply, and she raised her gaze, frowning at the look on Caleb's face.

"What?"

"Are you sure?" he asked.

"Of course," she said.

"There's doubt in your voice," he said.

She swallowed and stared at the table in confusion. He was right. She could hear the doubt as well. But that was her being silly and emotional. Yes, her father was very fond of Frederick, and he spoke of him almost as if he were already his son-in-law, but the man had tried to violate her. As fond as her father was of Frederick, he loved his only child.

If Frederick convinces your father that it was not force? He can be very charming when he wants. What then? It is your word against his, and you're only a woman. If Frederick sways your father to his thinking, you'll be forced to marry him. You know that. Do you want someone like him taking your virginity?

No, she really didn't. Not after Caleb's touch, not after realizing that intimate kissing and touching could be so very pleasurable. A little shudder went through her at the thought of Frederick touching her the way Caleb had.

"Ellie? Are you feeling ill?" Caleb asked.

She suddenly felt tired and sick to her stomach and stood abruptly. "Would you mind if I used the daybed to lie down? I'm a bit tired, and my stomach is queasy."

"It's too cold in that room," he said, "and the daybed is uncomfortable. Use my bed."

"Oh no, I can't do that," she said nervously.

"I insist," he said, giving her another warm smile. "You're

my guest, and I want you to be comfortable. I will remain in the living room until you wake from your nap. You have my word."

She licked her lips before nodding. "Th-thank you, Caleb. I appreciate your kindness."

"It's my pleasure, Ellie. Call for me if you need anything. All right?"

"Yes, thank you again."

She stood, held the quilt up so it didn't drag on the floor, and disappeared into the bedroom.

CHAPTER 3

C aleb brought in the tub and melted buckets of snow until there was just enough for him to bathe in. He stripped and climbed into the tub. He bathed quickly, washing away the dirt and smell of the barn. He ran his fingers through his thick beard before trimming away the excess hair with scissors, then shaved his face smooth. It had been over a year since he had shaved, and seeing so much of his face again was a little odd. Ellie might have responded to his touch earlier, but he had a feeling he needed to smell better and look less wild if he intended to go through with his plan of seduction.

My darling, no. Please, no.

He ignored Missy's voice and climbed out of the tub. He dressed quickly and emptied and rinsed the tub before bringing in more buckets of snow. He heated them on the woodstove and paced back and forth in the kitchen. It was over three hours since Ellie had disappeared into the bedroom, and he wondered if he should knock on the door. She was rather pale when she asked to lie down. Talking about what the banker had tried to do to her had upset her badly.

He felt a moment of anger toward a man he had never formally met. What kind of man would take a woman against her will? Just the thought of forcing Ellie into fucking made him feel nauseous. She was so fragile and rather sweet – the man had to be a monster to take what she didn't want to give freely.

What if she doesn't want to give you her innocence, my darling? Will you continue with your plan?

Of course, I won't, he snapped at the voice that served as Missy. *But she does want me – that was apparent this morning. It won't take much to make her mine.*

No, I suppose it will not.

I'm doing this for you, Missy. That man took you from me, and he deserves to suffer.

I am dead, my darling. My bones are turning to dust – what do I care if he suffers? You do this for you, not for me.

Fine, I do it for me. He should suffer the way I have.

And what of the girl? What has she ever done to you?

The girl will be fine. Her father will still love her. She's his daughter, for God's sake.

Yet you would see her remain unmarried for the rest of her life for the sake of your revenge?

She will find a husband. I will only take her once and won't teach her how to please a man. It will be easy enough for her to fake her innocence on her wedding night.

You sound like a madman, my darling. Do you not hear it?

When I have my revenge, the madness will ease.

The water was beginning to bubble, and he carried the buckets to the tub and poured them in. The bedroom door opened, and Ellie emerged. She still looked pale, but the dark circles under her eyes had disappeared, and her mouth dropped open as she stared at him.

"What's wrong?" He asked.

"I – you look different without your beard."

He smiled at her, and she shifted the quilt closer to her body. "I figured it was time for the beard to go."

"Oh," she said. "I'm sorry for sleeping so long."

"It's fine. You needed your rest," he said. "Are you hungry?"

She shook her head, and he frowned slightly. The woman really didn't eat enough. "It's past lunch. Are you sure you don't want something to eat?"

"I'm sure," she said as she eyed the steaming tub. "Are you having a bath?"

"I bathed earlier. This is for you."

"Really?" Her face lit up, and he nodded.

"Yes. I thought you would enjoy a warm bath."

"I would, I really would," she said eagerly. "Thank you so much, Caleb."

"It's my pleasure, Ellie," he said warmly.

He finished filling the tub, and she dipped her hand into the water.

"You may want to let it cool a bit," he advised.

She shook her head. "No, it's perfect. I'm still a little cold. In fact, I worried that I would never be warm again."

He studied her bare feet, feeling a twinge of guilt for not even giving her a pair of socks. He squashed the sentiment firmly before smiling again at her. "The soap and towels are next to the tub. I'll retire to the bedroom to give you privacy. Call me when you're finished."

"Thank you again." She gave him a warm smile that made his conscience twinge again, and he nodded before walking to the bedroom. He closed the door and sat on the bed before leaning over and inhaling. He could smell her scent on the sheets, and it sent a little trickle of lust through him. She really was an attractive woman. While he never thought he would be attracted to a woman as timid as she was, the mental image of her naked and wet was making his groin stir. He ignored it grimly and lay down on the bed, staring blankly at the ceiling as the wind howled.

* * *

ELLIE RINSED HER HAIR A FINAL TIME BEFORE RELAXING IN THE tub. She had soaked in the hot water until it started to cool, then quickly washed her hair and her body. Despite the cooling water, she wanted to linger in the tub, but Caleb would grow impatient in the bedroom. It was getting close to dinner, and he probably had evening chores. She didn't know much about farming but knew they lived busy and difficult lives.

She closed her eyes for a moment. When she had stepped out of the bedroom and seen Caleb with his too-long hair combed and that horridly bushy beard gone, she felt the same rush of pleasure in her belly from this morning in his bed. She had thought him to be unattractive but free of the hair covering most of his face – he was a very handsome man. He had nice, full lips and a strong jaw, and she was fascinated by the slight indent in his chin. Frederick's chin was nearly non-existent, and his carefully waxed mustache was rather unappealing to her.

Without the beard, Caleb looked oddly familiar to her. Had she met him before? It was entirely possible. Her father was well-known in the town, and they were often stopped and spoken to by others. She closed her eyes and concentrated. A memory of a woman with blonde hair and a pretty blue dress tugged at her, but it slipped away before it could take firm hold in her mind.

She thought again about Caleb's lips, how they felt when they touched her mouth and pulled on her nipples, and another surge of pleasure went through her body. Her nipples hardened, and she closed her eyes and took a few deep breaths. She had no idea what was happening to her. Her reaction to his touch was incredibly shameful but nearly impossible to control. She wanted his touch again. She wanted to know what kissing those firm lips unencumbered by a beard was like.

Ellie, stop! You're acting like a painted woman! Have some self-control.

She climbed out of the tub and quickly dried off with the rough towel. She glanced at her chemise. She didn't want to put it back on her clean skin. She wrapped the quilt around her body and walked nervously to the bedroom door.

She knocked lightly and stumbled back when the door opened immediately. Her foot caught on the edge of the quilt, and she would have fallen if Caleb hadn't caught her with a quickness that surprised her. His strong arm was wrapped around her waist, and he studied her wet hair before his gaze dropped to her mouth. She licked her suddenly dry lips, and his eyes turned from the light blue of a calm ocean to the dark blue of a stormy one.

"Ellie?" he said hoarsely. "Did you hurt yourself?"

"N-no," she stuttered. "But I wondered if I could borrow a shirt. My clothes are still damp, and my chemise isn't clean."

He was still holding her around the waist, and she was too aware of his hand on her hip.

"Of course," he said. He released her, and she swallowed her disappointment as he disappeared into the bedroom. He returned with a shirt and a pair of thick wool socks.

"Here," he said a bit gruffly. "The floors are too cold for bare feet."

"Thank you," she said gratefully.

There was an uncomfortable silence before Caleb cleared

his throat. "I'm going out to do evening chores. Leave the water in the tub. I'll empty it when I return."

She nodded and watched silently as he put on his jacket and boots and whistled for Scout. The dog was lying beside the fireplace but jumped eagerly to his feet and followed Caleb out into the storm.

* * *

CALEB RETURNED TO THE WARM HOUSE ALMOST AN HOUR later. He inhaled deeply as the smell of roasting meat drifted to him. Ellie was standing in the kitchen at the wood stove. She was wearing just his shirt and socks, and he studied her firm backside for a moment before removing his outerwear.

"I found your icebox and the door to the root cellar," she said shyly. "I thought I would start dinner. I hope you don't mind."

"You can cook?" He asked.

She laughed. "Yes. Does that surprise you?"

"A little," he said.

"My mother loved to cook, and she taught me at a young age," she said. "I'm not the best cook, but I enjoy it."

"Anything you make will be better than what I attempt," he said with a small grin.

He emptied the tub as she moved about the kitchen. She seemed completely at ease, searching the cupboards for dishes and setting the table. She had braided her dark hair, and it hung nearly to her waist. As he sat at the table, he found himself fascinated by how it gleamed in the candlelight.

Scout placed his head on his knee and scratched the dog's head absentmindedly as he watched Ellie dish up the food. He had to admit it was nice to come in from the chores to a woman cooking his dinner.

Don't, Caleb. Don't start thinking that Ellie belongs here. She doesn't.

No, she didn't. He was playing a game, and it would be wise for him to remember that.

She sat across from him and passed the bowl of steaming potatoes to him. "Dig in."

"It smells delicious," he said as he scooped potatoes onto his plate before taking the meat platter.

"Hopefully, it tastes delicious as well," she said with a soft smile.

"I'm sure it will, Ellie." He lowered his voice and briefly allowed his gaze to drift down to her chest.

Her soft flush assured him it had not gone unnoticed, and she dropped her fork nervously. It clattered against her plate, and she winced. "Sorry."

"It's fine." He took a helping of carrots before handing them to her.

They ate silently for a few moments before he smiled at her. "This is really good."

"I'm glad you're enjoying it," she said.

He was relieved she was eating a good amount and immediately berated himself. What did he care how much she ate? As long as she had enough strength to sleep with him, she could starve for all he cared.

After finishing the meal, he fed Scout before helping her with the dishes. He stood a little closer than necessary, letting his arm brush against hers as he dried. He was pleased to see she was flushed again by the time they were finished. He sat on the sofa, hiding his disappointment when she didn't join him but sat on the floor close to the fire.

"The sofa is more comfortable," he said.

"I'm a bit cold again," she said apologetically.

He watched silently as she unbraided her hair and ran her fingers through it. It was tangled from her bath, and she winced a little as she tried to comb it out. After a moment, he stood and disappeared into the bedroom. He returned with a wide-toothed comb, and she gave him a nervous look when he pulled a chair behind her.

"Wh-what are you doing?"

"Hold still," he instructed before combing her hair. He pulled gently at the tangles as she sat stiffly.

"Caleb, you don't - "

"I don't mind," he said.

He didn't mind. He had brushed Missy's hair for her nearly every night, and he found it almost soothing to resurrect this small and intimate ritual. Ellie's hair was incredibly soft, and he combed it long after the tangles were gone. She was relaxing, resting her back against his shins, as she stared silently into the fire. He set the comb on his lap and ignored his half-hard cock as he gathered her hair in his hands. She twitched when she felt his fingers against her scalp but didn't say anything. He quickly braided her hair before holding his hand out for the piece of ribbon she held. She handed it to him without speaking, and he tied it around the end of her hair.

"Thank you, Caleb," she whispered.

"You're welcome."

Her body was shivering despite the warmth of the fire, and he stood as she glanced nervously at him. He blew out all the candles but one before carrying it to where she still sat in front of the fire. "We should go to bed, Ellie."

She gave him a wide-eyed look of anxiety. "Oh, right. I'll sleep in the other bedroom."

He shook his head. "That room will be freezing by now, and it's only going to grow colder through the night."

"The sofa," she said with a tinge of desperation. "I can sleep on the sofa."

"It's too uncomfortable." He held out his hand and gave her a slightly impatient look. "Let's go, Ellie."

"I can't sleep in the same bed with you. It isn't proper," she whispered.

"We slept together last night," he said.

Her cheeks turned red, and she stared at the floor. He took her hand and tugged her to her feet.

"Don't worry, Ellie. I won't do anything improper," he said.

"I – do you promise?" she whispered.

"Yes," he lied. "Join me in my bed. You'll need me to keep you warm."

"I really would rather sleep on the sofa," she said.

He shook his head. "No, Ellie. You'll be too cold. Come with me."

He walked toward the bedroom, secretly thrilled when she followed without protesting. He would have given in to her request if she had asked to sleep on the sofa again. As it was, his plan to seduce her the moment they were in the bed wasn't going to work. She was much too anxious to feel any need for him. Her earlier desire for him had disappeared, and he swallowed down his anxiety. If the blizzard ended before he could convince her to let him fuck her, he would lose his chance. He supposed he could put off returning her to her home for another day or so after the blizzard ended, but it was risky. She would want to leave and might even try to leave on her own.

They were in the bedroom now, and he set the candle on the nightstand before stripping off his shirt and pants. Ellie's cheeks were bright red. He could see the blush even in the soft glow of the candle. Keeping his socks on, she climbed into the bed and yanked the covers to her chin before turning her back to him. She curled into a little ball as he hooked his hands in the waistband of his drawers before changing his mind. He usually slept naked, but it would ease Ellie's anxiety if he weren't completely naked. He climbed into the bed and blew out the candle before turning on his side to face Ellie's back.

"Good night, Caleb," she said softly before squirming to the edge of the bed.

"Good night, Ellie."

He lay quietly for the next half hour as her shaking increased. It was just as cold in this bedroom as in the other, but he was hot-blooded, and the sheets and thick blankets were enough to keep him warm. Ellie, on the other hand, was obviously freezing. When her teeth chattered, he wrapped his arm around her waist and pulled her back against him.

She tried to squirm away. "Caleb, you said you wouldn't be improper with me."

"I'm only trying to keep you warm," he said patiently. "You're freezing, Ellie."

"I'm fine," she protested. "I don't need you to keep me warm."

"I'm very tired, and I'll never fall asleep with your teeth chattering so loudly." He allowed a hint of impatience into his voice. "Let me hold you until you're warm."

"I'm sorry," she said. "I don't mean to keep you awake."

"I know," he said. "Just relax."

"You are very warm," she said hesitantly.

He laughed softly and pulled her closer until her ass was pressed snugly against his pelvis. "It's a blessing in the winter and a curse in the summer."

She gave in and relaxed against him. "Thank you, Caleb. You're being very kind."

Guilt flooded through him, and his arm tightened around her waist. "Go to sleep, Ellie."

He planned to wait until she fell asleep before beginning to touch her. He would have her aroused and wanting him before she was fully awake. She was so responsive to his touch that he had no doubt of his ability to coax her into giving him her innocence. But as the minutes ticked by and Ellie's breathing slowed and deepened, he also began to feel sleepy. There was something comforting about Ellie's slender body pressed against his. She was no longer cold, thanks to his body heat. A feeling of contentment washed over him for the first time in two years. The wind was howling and moaning, and the bedroom was freezing, but their combined body heat kept the bed toasty warm. He couldn't deny that he enjoyed having a warm woman in his bed again. The winter nights were long and cold on the prairies, and it felt good to have a woman pressed against him, even if it was the daughter of the man he hated.

Shh, my darling. Sleep.

Yes, he thought tiredly. Missy was right – sleep was needed and not just for him. Ellie was clearly still exhausted by her ordeal. He felt a moment of protectiveness that would have made him extremely nervous if he were fully awake. His drowsiness only made it seem vaguely right to be protective of her, and he pulled her even closer before cupping one full breast and burying his face in the back of her neck.

* * *

WHEN HE WOKE, IT WAS CLOSE TO DAWN. THE BLIZZARD STILL raged outside, but it wasn't as dark in the bedroom, and his internal clock assured him it was nearly time to wake. He cursed to himself. He had meant to seduce Ellie in the night, and instead, he had fallen asleep.

He paused when he felt her warm mouth press against his throat. She had turned in her sleep. Her body was flattened against his, and her arm was wrapped firmly around his waist. He pulled experimentally on her bare thigh, a grin crossing his face when she allowed him to lift it and slip his leg between hers. She pressed her mouth against his throat again, and he lifted his chin. She was half-asleep, but it didn't stop her from tasting his skin with her soft, pink tongue.

He groaned as his cock went from half-mast to fully erect. It pushed against Ellie's flat abdomen, and she made her own quiet groan before rubbing her body against his. Hell, seducing her would be easier than he thought. She might be a virgin, but her body was ripe and willing for his.

She lifted her head and blinked sleepily at him before a soft smile crossed her lips. "Good morning, Caleb."

"Good morning, Ellie," he said quietly.

He jerked in surprise when she pressed her mouth against his but quickly took control of the kiss. He slid his tongue between her lips, and she returned his kiss eagerly as he cupped her breast through his shirt. He could feel her nipple hardening against his palm, and with an impatient growl, he quickly unbuttoned her shirt and tugged it open. He rolled her to her back and pushed down the covers to study her naked body.

God, she was beautiful. Her skin was the colour of milk, and he watched her pink nipples harden in the cold air before letting his gaze fall to the dark curls between her thighs. Her legs were parted, and he was about to cup her pussy when her fingers gripped his broad shoulders.

She was wide awake now as his cock stirred against her leg. Her cheeks were stained red, and her eyes were wide with embarrassment and lust.

"Caleb, you – you promised," she said.

"You started it, my sweet," he said in a low voice. "I'm just giving you what you want."

"I didn't start anything," she said.

He laughed before cupping her breast and pulling on her

nipple. "I woke to find you kissing me and rubbing your body against mine."

She groaned with embarrassment, and he dipped his head and suckled at her nipple until she was gasping and squirming.

"Don't be embarrassed. It's natural for your body to react this way," he said before kissing her deeply.

She clutched at his naked back as he kissed her and continued to tease her nipples with his fingers.

"I want to make you feel good, Ellie. Will you let me?"

"It isn't proper," she gasped.

He tweaked her nipple, liking the way it made her back arch, and her thighs widen even further before trailing kisses over her neck and upper chest.

"It's proper," he said. "You want me, and I want you. There's nothing wrong with that."

"Caleb," she moaned. "I don't understand what's happening to me."

"Your body needs to be touched, sweetheart," he said. "You need me to make you feel good. Let me, Ellie."

She hesitated before nodding, and he smiled at her and kissed her lightly. "Relax, sweetheart."

He bent his head and kissed and nipped at her full breasts before capturing one nipple between his teeth. He worried it lightly with his lips and teeth until she was arching her back and making soft moans of pleasure that had his cock straining against her thigh.

He pressed his hand between her thighs. She was soaking wet, and he felt an odd tingle of pride that he could make someone like her want someone like him.

Oh yes, my darling. Making the sweet little rich girl want the poor farmer just so he can destroy her life is something to be proud of, Missy said dryly.

Get out of my head! he snapped at her and sighed with relief when she retreated.

"Caleb?" Ellie's voice was low and hesitant. "Is – is there something wrong?"

He smiled at her before shaking his head. "No, you're perfect, Ellie."

She blushed and then gasped loudly when he ran his fingers over her swollen clit. She clutched at his arms as he stroked the sensitive bundle of nerves again.

He could take her now. She was wet and more than ready for him. He could bury his cock deep in her body, find the relief he was suddenly aching for, and she wouldn't ask him to stop. She might come from being fucked, some women could, but did it matter if she did or not? She wouldn't know the difference. She wouldn't know what it was like to orgasm, and perhaps would be better for her if she didn't. It would help her lie about her innocence if her husband was the first to show her the pleasure of an orgasm. His stomach clenched oddly at the thought of another man touching her, of another man hearing her soft cries and moans of pleasure, and his fingers slowed against her clit.

She immediately made a soft mewling noise of need and clutched again at his shoulders. "Oh please, Caleb. Please don't stop."

He stared at her flushed face and heaving chest before rubbing her clit again. He couldn't leave her unsatisfied, even if he were only fucking her as a way to take his revenge. Nothing pleased him more in bed than watching a woman climax, and there would be no harm in bringing her to orgasm just once.

He pushed his middle finger into her tight entrance. She tensed, and he kissed her soothingly before rubbing her clit with his thumb. "Relax, sweetheart. I'm going to make you feel good, remember?"

She moaned at his touch, and he moved his finger in and out of her as he rubbed firmly at her clit. Her head was beginning to thrash on the pillow, and her nails dug into his back as her pelvis arched against his hand. He watched with a small smile on his face as her body stiffened, and she made a loud shriek of pleasure. Wetness coated his hand, and she shook with the intensity of her orgasm.

"Oh," she whispered repeatedly, "oh, oh, oh."

His smile widened, and he gave her a few moments to recover before moving between her legs. She gave him a sweet little smile that made his chest tighten.

"That felt so good, Caleb."

Her eyes drifted shut, and he palmed her breast before placing his cock at the entrance to her pussy. He frowned when she tensed immediately, and an anxious look crossed her face.

* * *

ELLIE COULDN'T BELIEVE HOW GOOD SHE FELT. CALEB'S WARM touch had sent indescribable pleasure through her entire body, and she was warm and delightfully relaxed. The ache between her thighs was gone for the first time since she had allowed Caleb to touch her yesterday morning. Caleb was moving beside her, his big body nudging her thighs apart. She spread them willingly and smiled at him when he kneeled between her legs.

"That felt so good, Caleb."

She closed her eyes as his big hand squeezed her breast lightly. The head of his cock probed at her pussy, and a sudden jolt of apprehension shot through her. She tensed and immediately berated herself. She wanted this, so why was she suddenly feeling so anxious?

Because it's going to hurt. Because you barely know the man?

41

Because you're allowing someone who isn't your husband to take your virginity? Pick a reason, Ellie.

She shut out her inner voice. She wanted Caleb, and he had made her feel so good. It was only right that she returned the favour. Besides, if she gave him her virginity, there would be no worry that her father would force her to marry Frederick. If he believed Frederick over her, she would simply tell him she was no longer innocent and that Frederick would no longer want her.

You would use Caleb in such a manner? He saved your life and has been nothing but kind to you.

She ignored her feelings of guilt. Caleb wouldn't care about her reasons for sleeping with him. Besides, he would never know her true intention for allowing him to take her.

Her eyes opened in a hurry when Caleb moved off her and sat on the side of the bed. Clutching his shirt closed, she sat up and touched his back timidly.

"Caleb? What did I do wrong?"

"Nothing," he said hoarsely. "It's getting late, and the animals need to be fed."

Without looking at her, he dressed and left the bedroom. Her cheeks burning with embarrassment, she slid off the bed and hurried after him. He was already in his jacket and boots, and he ignored her when she called his name. With Scout at his heels, he left the house.

She blinked back the sudden tears. Obviously, she had done something wrong, but for the life of her she couldn't figure out what. She hurried to the fireplace. The fire was low, and she built it up quickly before picking up her clothes. They were finally dry, and she hesitated before leaving her corset and petticoats. They were wildly uncomfortable, and besides, Caleb had already seen her completely naked. What did it matter if she wore only her dress around him?

She slipped into her skirt and bodice before folding his shirt neatly and placing it back in the bedroom. She would ask him later about gathering some snow to melt for laundry.

A particularly strong gust of wind rocked the house, and she shivered before moving to the kitchen. She had disappointed Caleb in the bedroom but would do her best to make up for it by making him a nice breakfast.

* * *

CALEB LEANED HIS HEAD AGAINST RUBY'S WARM SIDE. SHE mooed contently as he milked her, and he closed his eyes for a moment. What was wrong with him? He had exactly what he wanted and ran like a frightened child instead of taking Ellie.

Anger began to edge out his confusion. Why had he stopped? If the blizzard ended today, he would not get another chance. It was Ellie's fault, he decided. His moment of weakness came about because of her obvious anxiety. She wasn't ready for him to take her, despite her willingness to be touched. If he had taken her this morning, she might have thought him to be like Frederick, which made his stomach curl.

He swore softly. He was a fool. Ellie wanted him, and her moment of anxiety was nothing more than nerves. He should have taken what he wanted and been done with her.

Perhaps, my darling, that's the real reason you stopped. You don't want to be done with her. Deep down, you know you'll want more once you've been with her.

Bullshit, he hissed at Missy's voice. *Once I've fucked her, I'll have no further use for her.*

He finished milking Ruby and fed the horses and the chickens before gathering the eggs. He would return to the house and finish what he had started earlier. Ellie's virginity would belong to him before the day was done.

When he returned to the house, Ellie was wearing her dress and cooking breakfast. He inhaled the good smell of cooking ham before moving to the wash basin. He washed up quickly and joined Ellie in the kitchen. She stared studiously at the cooking meat, and he made his voice gentle and apologetic.

"I'm sorry for earlier, Ellie."

"You don't need to apologize," she said quickly. "It was all my fault. I'm sorry for being so forward with you."

"I didn't mind," he said.

"Then," she gave him a timid look, "why did you leave before we…"

She trailed off with her cheeks flushing, and he cleared his throat. "I told you it was getting late, and the animals needed to be fed."

"Right, of course," she said as she blinked rapidly.

He sighed loudly. "You did nothing wrong. I promise."

She nodded, and his stomach churning, he said, "I am not looking for a wife, Ellie. It would be wrong of me to take you when I do not intend to marry you. You are too fragile and delicate to be a farmer's wife."

What happened to her virginity would be yours by the end of the day? His inner voice asked.

Bloody hell. What was wrong with him? Why the hell did he say that to her? It had popped out before he could stop it, and he could hear Missy's soft murmur of approval in his head.

He groaned when Ellie began to cry softly. He hesitated before patting her back gingerly. "Please don't cry, Ellie."

"What you must think of me," she sobbed. "I'm acting like a – a painted woman, and I don't know why or what's wrong with me!"

She was really sobbing now, and he fished his handker-chief out of his pocket and pressed it into her hand. She wiped her cheeks as he awkwardly patted her back again.

"There's nothing wrong with you, Ellie," he said. "Your reaction to being touched and kissed is perfectly normal. I promise."

"Do you mean it?" she whispered. "Or do you secretly think terribly of me?"

She was still crying, and he pulled her into his embrace, rubbing her back lightly as she rested her head on his broad chest.

"I do not. Your reaction to my touch is very," he paused, "pleasing to me."

"But you don't want me," she whispered.

"I do," he said dryly. "Trust me on that."

"I want you too," she whispered again.

He blew his breath out. Now was the time to take her back to his bed. He opened his mouth and said, "I want to fuck you, Ellie. You have no idea how much I want that, but I can't. I won't take advantage of you."

Fool! What are you doing? His inner voice said indignantly.

"But, I -"

"Enough, Ellie," he said gently, and she nodded in defeat before squirming out of his embrace.

She wiped the lingering tears from her face and straight-ened her back before saying briskly, "Breakfast is almost ready."

He returned to his chair, studying the plate before him as she moved quietly about the kitchen.

CHAPTER 4

Ellie stared at the bowl of stew in front of her. After breakfast, she made fresh bread and a pot of stew for their midday meal. She needed to keep busy and do something to help her ignore the growing tension between them. But even though the food smelled delicious, she couldn't eat. She managed to force down a few bites of food at breakfast, but eating now was impossible.

Her stomach was churning with nerves and anxiety and - she closed her eyes briefly - need. She needed Caleb badly and despite what he had said earlier, he was having difficulty controlling his own need for her. She could see it in the tenseness of his body and in the way his gaze lingered on her breasts and pelvis. It was all she could do not to take his hand and lead him to the bedroom.

Why aren't you then? You could override his protests easily enough.

Because a proper lady didn't –

Forget being proper, her mind snapped. *You can deny it all you want, but you know deep down that your father will side with Frederick. It isn't that he doesn't love you. He just believes that*

Frederick will be a good provider. He will accept Frederick's word over yours, and as much as that hurts, you need to accept it and move forward with your plan to seduce Caleb.

She almost laughed out loud. Seduce Caleb? She was a virgin, for God's sake. What did she know of seduction?

You know more than you think. Besides, it won't take much – the man's cock has been straining at his pants all morning.

She shied away from her mind's coarse language even though it brought a surge of wetness between her thighs. It was true. More than once, she had caught sight of the bulge in the front of his trousers and - God help her - it made her wet and aching every single time.

Forget that you're attracted to him – that happens to be a bonus. You really need to concentrate on figuring out a way to escape being married to Frederick, and the man sitting across from you is your best chance. Seduce him into taking your virginity, and your problem with Frederick will be finished.

It isn't right, she argued. *It isn't right to use Caleb in such a manner and –*

Stop! Would you rather be married to Frederick, spend every night in his bed while he touches you with his vile hands and mouth, or spend one night with a man who you want desperately and makes you feel things you didn't think possible? When you find the man you will marry, lying about your innocence will be easy enough.

Caleb knew! He knew right away that I was a virgin. If it were that easy for him, another man would be able to tell when I am no longer a virgin.

Not likely. Most men are not like Caleb. They are easily distracted by a woman's touch and the feel of her body. Stop feeling guilty and do what has to be done, you silly little girl!

She was dismayed at her inner voice's cold, calculating tone, but it was right. Her father would believe Frederick over her. She was sure of it. Since her virginity seemed so precious to the vile man, she could think of only one way to end his interest in her.

"You need to eat, Ellie," Caleb said.

She squeezed her eyes shut, took a deep breath and plastered what she hoped was an inviting smile on her face. "I'm not hungry for food."

His nostrils flared, and the dark look of lust he gave her took her breath away. "Caleb, I - "

"I'm going to lie down for a while. I have a headache," he said.

He stood abruptly, and she had a brief glimpse of that bulge at the front of his pants again before he strode to the bedroom and slammed the door shut.

She waited five minutes before walking to the bedroom and quietly easing open the door. Her breath caught in her throat. Caleb was standing naked at the window. His head was down, and his left hand was braced against the wall as his right arm moved in a hurried, jerking motion. She wasn't entirely certain what he was doing, but her body didn't care. Just seeing him naked brought wetness to her core, and her pelvis ached as she stepped into the room and shut the door.

Without looking at her, he said, "Go away, Ellie."

She unbuttoned her bodice before walking to him and pressing her naked breasts against his warm back. He made a low guttural noise of need, and the sound sent shivers down her back.

She peeked around his side, staring at his penis. It was long and thick, and the head of it was leaking a clear fluid. He wrapped his hand around it and stroked it firmly as she watched.

"Does that feel good?" she whispered.

"Please leave," he groaned.

She slipped in front of him and pressed her body against his, trapping his hand and his cock against the soft folds of her skirt. He stared hungrily at her naked breasts. She tugged his left hand away from the wall and placed it on her breast. He squeezed it roughly, rubbing his thumb over her hard nipple. She made an encouraging moan before reaching between them and wrapping her small hand over his large one.

"Let me touch you," she murmured.

He hesitated and then dropped his hand. She curved her fingers around the thick length of his shaft and stroked back and forth like he had done. The skin was velvety smooth beneath her palm, and she marveled inwardly at the hardness of it as he groaned again and his hips bucked against her.

"Ellie," he groaned. "Ellie, please. You need to stop. You need to - "

She squeezed him firmly, and he made a hoarse shout of pleasure. His head fell back, and the cords stood out in his neck as his entire body shook. Warm liquid covered her hand and the front of her skirt. She continued to stroke him until he pulled her hand away with a harsh tug.

"Why are you doing this to me?" he muttered.

"Because I want to make you feel as good as you made me feel," she said. "Did I, Caleb? Did you like it when I touched you?"

"Yes," he said. "I want you. I want to take you to my bed and feel your tight little pussy wrapped around my cock."

She blushed at his coarseness but pressed her body even closer to his. "I want that too. Please, will you take me to your bed?"

"Are you sure?" he said hoarsely. "Are you absolutely sure that - "

"Yes," she said. "I want you."

Lust flared in his eyes, and she could feel his penis twitching against her. Without another word, he pulled her bodice down her arms and dropped it to the floor before tugging her skirt down her legs. He studied her naked body, and she squeaked in surprise when he suddenly lifted her and carried her to the bed. He dropped her onto it and covered her body with his.

He kissed her roughly, sliding his tongue deep into her mouth as she wrapped her legs around his waist and rubbed her pussy against him. He growled into her mouth before kissing his way to her breasts. He spent long moments licking and sucking at her nipples until her body was shuddering, and she was making loud moans of need. He kissed his way down her flat stomach, licking around her navel before nibbling at each of her hipbones.

When he stretched his body between her thighs, she raised her head and gave him a nervous look. "Caleb, what are you doing?"

He kissed her dark patch of curls in reply, and she jerked against him before pushing at his head. "Don't - don't do that. It isn't proper."

He ignored her protests and took her wrists. He held them tightly against her hips as she tried frantically to close her thighs. His large body kept them open, and she struggled to free herself when she felt his warm breath on the lips of her pussy.

"Caleb, you shouldn't - "

Her protest died on her lips as he licked her pussy.

"Oh," she said in a quiet voice. "Oh my goodness."

He chuckled, and the low sound sent a new surge of shivers down her back. He licked her again. "Your little pussy tastes good, sweetheart."

"Oh," she said again. It seemed to be the only thing she was capable of saying.

"Spread your legs, my sweet," he demanded. "Let me taste all of your pussy."

She spread her legs wide. Caleb kept her wrists clamped

tightly against her thighs despite her obvious submission, and she shrieked in delight at the first brush of his tongue against her swollen clit.

"Caleb!" Her pelvis arched up to meet his tongue as he nibbled lightly on the lips of her pussy.

"Caleb, please!" She begged when he kissed first one inner thigh, then the other.

"Do you want me to taste your pussy again, Ellie?" he teased lightly before licking her inner thigh.

"Yes!" she shouted. "Very much!"

He laughed, and she moaned again when he buried his face between her thighs and nibbled and kissed at her wet pussy lips. She writhed against him when he flicked her clit lightly with his tongue and then screamed when he sucked firmly on it. Her orgasm washed over her, and she bucked and shrieked and cried his name.

* * *

CALEB LICKED AWAY THE LAST OF ELLIE'S SWEET CREAM BEFORE studying her flushed face and shaking body. She was splayed out on the bed with her legs spread wide and her chest heaving for breath. He released her wrists and pressed his hands against the back of her thighs, lifting them up and out until she was completely open to him.

"Once more, I think," he murmured.

"What?" She said breathlessly. "What? No, I can't do that again. I can't - "

He slid his tongue into her narrow entrance. She gasped loudly and clutched at his head as he held her legs firmly in the air and took his time kissing and licking every part of her soaking wet pussy. He licked her clean again, relishing the taste of her on his tongue. He sucked on her clit, teasing the swollen nub with his tongue. It didn't take very long before she was coming again, moaning and writhing and screaming his name. God, he loved her reaction to his touch. He could spend hours making her climax.

"Caleb," she panted as he lowered her legs to the bed. "Please, Caleb, please."

He moved until he was kneeling between her legs and rubbed her flat stomach. "Are you ready for me, sweetheart?"

"Yes, oh yes," she moaned.

He positioned his cock at her entrance, watching her face for any signs of tension or distress. She opened her eyes and smiled hazily at him. "Please. I want you so much."

He leaned over her and, as he pushed his cock deep into her pussy, swallowed her cry of pain with his mouth. She squeezed her hands around his biceps, her body trembling beneath him as he kissed her again and again and forced his body to stay perfectly still.

"I'm sorry," he whispered.

She touched his face with the tips of her fingers, stroking them lightly across the dark stubble. "It's fine. The pain is fading."

Her body was still tense, and he waited until she had relaxed and her legs weren't pressed so tightly against his hips. She moved experimentally below him, and he groaned loudly, his pelvis jerking against hers.

"Ellie," he moaned. "I need to move."

She kissed him softly, cupping his face with her warm hands and arched her pelvis against his. He moaned again and forced himself to move slowly within her. He watched her face as he moved, and she gave him a shy look.

"Does it feel good?"

"So good," he muttered. "Your little pussy is so tight and warm, sweetheart. You have no idea how good it feels."

She flushed prettily before pushing her pelvis tentatively at him. Their hips slapped together awkwardly until she found his rhythm, and he praised her softly, making her flush again with pleasure.

"Good, my sweet," he praised her again. "Wrap your legs around my waist."

She did as he asked, and he pushed in and out with firm strokes. His balls were tightening, and his cock was swelling, and he reached between them and rubbed lightly at her clit.

"Oh my goodness!" She said, and he couldn't stop his wide grin.

He rubbed firmly, trying to keep his rhythm steady within her, but after only a few moments, it was nearly impossible. She had lost their bodies' rhythm completely as her orgasm grew close, and she rocked and bucked against him until, with a soft cry, she came again. Her pussy clenched down around him, squeezing tightly, and he groaned and buried his face in her warm neck before giving in to the urge to climax. Warm seed poured out of him, coating her insides and marking her as his, and he collapsed against her slender body. He kissed her damp skin as she rubbed his broad back. After a few moments, he rolled off of her and pulled her into his embrace. She stared sleepily at him, and he pressed a kiss against her forehead.

"Are you tired, Ellie?"

She nodded and closed her eyes, burrowing closer to him as he cupped one firm breast and whispered, "Go to sleep, sweetheart."

* * *

ELLIE STIRRED HER BOWL OF STEW BEFORE NIBBLING AT THE piece of bread. It stuck like glue in her throat and she swallowed with difficulty before sipping at her glass of water. When she woke up, Caleb had already left the bed. A basin of steaming hot water was sitting on the dresser, and she was thankful for his thoughtfulness. She was a little sore and sticky and she had gently washed away the evidence of Caleb taking her innocence. She had emerged from the bedroom to see Caleb sitting in the living room, staring into the fire. Although he was pleasant enough for the entire afternoon, she had no appetite for dinner.

He no longer wanted her. The bold looks and light touches he had bestowed on her before they slept together were gone. He had taken what he wanted from her, and that was it.

So? You took what you wanted from him, too, remember? Why should you be upset that he has done the same?

That was true, but unfortunately, she still wanted him. Even though she had successfully seduced him into taking her virginity, she wanted more. She wanted to touch him again, wanted him to touch her despite the soreness between her legs, and her feelings were hurt that he no longer seemed interested.

You don't know that for sure. You know nothing about the man.

Another good point. She cleared her throat and smiled warmly at him across the table. "Do you have any siblings, Caleb?"

"Yes. I have four brothers and two sisters. They're back east. Although the last letter I received from my younger brother suggested he was thinking of joining me here in the west."

"That would be nice for you to have family around," she said.

"It would be. How about you? Do you have any siblings?"

"No. I'm an only child. I've always wished for brothers and sisters, but my mother had several miscarriages after me and then never became pregnant again. It's hard on my father - he always wanted a son."

She hesitated, "How long were you married?"

"Six years."

He ate another bite of stew as she asked, "What was your wife's name?"

"Missy."

"That's a pretty name."

He didn't reply and she cleared her throat. "May I ask how she died?"

He shook his head. "I don't want to talk about it."

"Of course," she said hurriedly. "I'm sorry for being so personal, Caleb."

"It's fine."

"I think I may have met her once."

"You did," he confirmed. "In the general store."

"She was wearing a blue dress," Ellie said quietly.

He nodded, and she cast about for something else to say. "So, do you like to read?"

He glanced at her, and she pointed to the bookshelf. "You have lots of books."

"I do like reading. I don't have much time in the warmer months, but it passes the time in the winter."

"What type of crops do you grow?"

"Wheat," he said.

"I've always admired farmers and miners," she said quietly. "They often have challenging lives, but the ones I have met seem so happy and content."

He snorted loudly. "I doubt your father has many friends who are farmers."

"No, I suppose he doesn't, but I met some in town when they came to my father's clinic."

"They must be rich farmers if your father agreed to treat them," he suddenly said.

She frowned at the bitterness in his voice. "What do you mean?"

"Nothing," he muttered before standing and scraping the

last of his stew into Scout's bowl.

"Caleb, did I say something wrong?" she asked.

He shook his head. "No. I'm just very tired."

"Perhaps we should go to bed?" she asked timidly. Her heart was pounding, and her mouth was suddenly dry.

He nodded, but the tingle of excitement growing in her belly died when he said, "I think it would be best if you slept in the other bedroom tonight, Ellie. I'll give you plenty of extra blankets."

He stared fixedly at Scout eating the leftover stew, and she blinked back the hot tears before saying, "Of course."

He glanced at her before dropping his gaze back to Scout. "If you get too cold in the night, just - "

"I won't," she said. "I don't believe it's nearly as cold as last night. Perhaps we will wake in the morning to find the blizzard is over, and I can return home."

"Perhaps," he said.

"You will be happy to have your house back to yourself, I'm certain," she said.

He rubbed his forehead before scowling at the floor and disappearing into his bedroom. He reappeared with a stack of blankets and placed them in the second bedroom before striding back to his own. He stood in the doorway with his hands in tight fists before nodding in her direction. "Good night, Ellie."

"Good night, Caleb. Thank you again for everything."

She was very proud of how cheerful she sounded. She obviously was terrible in bed and had not pleased him at all, but she would be damned if she'd let him see how much his rejection hurt her. Besides, it was better this way. The less she knew about pleasing a man in bed – the better. It would make things easier with her future husband if she remained clueless about bedroom activities.

You mean he'll believe your lie more willingly. What kind of woman lies to her future husband about her sexual experience?

The kind of woman who didn't want to marry a violator, that was who. It didn't matter – what was done was done, and she couldn't take it back. She didn't want to anyway. Regardless of how Caleb felt about their time in bed together, it was extremely pleasant for her and she would never forget it.

* * *

CALEB SAT UP IN BED AND RAN HIS HANDS THROUGH HIS HAIR. He'd been in his room for nearly three hours and was entirely certain he wouldn't fall asleep. He couldn't fall asleep. He wanted Ellie too much.

He cursed softly and climbed out of bed to pace the room. He shouldn't want her. It was dangerous to even think about fucking her again, but Christ, if he didn't want to. It was all he could think about. Well, that and worrying that she was too cold in the other bedroom.

She probably is. You should bring her to your room and warm her.

Yes, he really should. There was no harm in helping Ellie to stay warm with his body heat. He could stop himself from touching her and from sinking his cock into her until she was moaning his name in a way that made his entire body tingle with pleasure.

Before he could change his mind, he left his bedroom and walked quickly to hers. He opened the door, shivering a little as the blast of cold air washed over his naked body. "Ellie? Come into my bedroom. It is too cold - "

Adrenaline surged through his veins. The bed was empty, and he felt a moment of pure panic. Ellie had left him. He sprinted to the front door as Scout whined loudly and joined him. She would never survive the blizzard. Why had he made her sleep in the other bedroom? She had given him a gift, and he had selfishly taken it and then tossed her aside like a piece of trash. No wonder she had chosen to leave rather than stay and be treated so badly. He was reaching for the door – he had forgotten completely about his nakedness – when he heard her soft voice.

"Caleb? What are you doing?"

He whirled around, straining to see in the dim light of the dying fire. Ellie was sitting in a nest of blankets on the floor in front of the fireplace, giving him a frightened look.

"What's wrong?" She clutched the blankets to her chest.

"What are you doing out here?" His fear made him gruff, and she shrank back as he stalked across the room and dropped to his knees beside her. He grabbed her arms and shook her lightly.

"You scared the hell out of me, Ellie! I thought you had left! Why aren't you in the bedroom?"

"I'm sorry," she said. "It was too cold in the bedroom, even with the extra blankets, so I decided to sleep by the fire. I didn't mean to worry you."

He cupped her head and glared at her. "You should have come to my bedroom if you were too cold. I would have warmed you."

"Y-you didn't want me in your bedroom," she stuttered. "I'm not stupid, Caleb. I know you don't want me anymore."

He kissed her hard on the mouth, thrusting his tongue between her lips as he wrapped his arm around her and pulled her flush against his chest. She was wearing his shirt again, and he unbuttoned it. She tugged her mouth away from his.

"What are you doing?"

"I do want you, Ellie. I want you so badly I can't sleep, I can't think – I'm going crazy."

He yanked off her shirt and leaned away so he could study her pale and naked body in the firelight. "You are so beautiful, sweetheart."

"Caleb," she said hesitantly, "it's okay if you don't want me anymore. I know I was, well, awkward in bed and I - "

He guided her hand to his erect cock. "Feel how much I want you."

She bit her bottom lip as her hand tightened around his cock, and she stroked him firmly. "I want you too."

"Good," he muttered before kissing her again. He pushed her onto her back in the blankets and knelt between her pale thighs. He was frantic for her and wanted nothing more than to be in her tight warmth. He forced himself to go slowly and rubbed her clit lightly with the tips of his fingers.

She moaned, her legs falling open as she arched into his touch, and he gave her an anxious look. "Are you too sore?"

She stared blankly at him for a moment before shaking her head. "No. Don't make me wait."

"Not yet, sweetheart," he groaned. "I don't want to hurt you again."

"You won't," she said, and he smiled a little at the impatience in her voice. "Caleb, I – I want to have sex with you again."

"Soon," he whispered before dipping his head and sucking at one stiff nipple.

She traced her fingers across his chest as he rubbed and stroked her clit until it was wet and swollen.

"Oh, Caleb, please," she suddenly begged.

Unable to deny her a moment longer, he pushed his cock deep into her warmth. Her pussy clung to him, her walls squeezing him so tightly he nearly climaxed. He pulled out in a hurry. She smacked him lightly on the chest and glared in frustration at him.

"Do not tease me a moment longer," she demanded.

He kissed her until she was breathless as he thrust lightly in and out of her.

"More," she moaned. "Please, I need more."

Her begging was driving his need to a fevered pitch, and he forgot his worry that she was sore and fucked her roughly. She cried his name, her hands dropping to grip his ass tightly as he thrust hard and deep.

His eyes widened in surprise when her body arched under his, and her pussy squeezed around him in an unmistakable sign of her orgasm. She shuddered wildly with her nails digging into his ass, and he shouted hoarsely before giving in to his own driving need to climax.

He buried his face into her neck, panting harshly as she rubbed his back before saying, "Will it always be this good?"

He studied her flushed face in the light of the fire and brushed away the strands of hair that had loosened from her braid. "With you? Yes."

She smiled shyly at him, and he couldn't help but press a kiss against her mouth. He stood, and her smile dropped from her face. "Are you going back to your room now?"

"Yes," he said before bending and picking her up, "and you're coming with me."

"I don't have to," she said uncertainly. "I'm warm enough by the fire."

He shook his head as he carried her to his room. "No, sweet Ellie. I want you in my bed."

CHAPTER 5

"Caleb, what time is it?"

She sat up in a hurry, staring blearily at him before pushing her hair out of her face.

"Early," he said as he pulled his shirt over his head. "I'm leaving to do the morning chores. Go back to sleep, sweetheart."

She yawned before giving him a sleepy smile. "I can't do that. I need to make your breakfast – you'll be hungry."

He pushed her back down onto the bed and covered her body with his. He kissed her and traced her lips with his tongue before giving her a playful grin. "The only thing I'll be hungry for is you, sweetheart. Go back to sleep. You'll need your rest for what I'll do to you when I'm done the chores."

She blushed fiercely, and he laughed before kissing the tip of her nose and leaving the bedroom.

When he returned, she had dozed off, and he quickly stripped and climbed into the bed beside her. He molded his cold body against her warm one. She muttered in discontent and tried to wiggle away. He held her firmly and cupped her breast, teasing her nipple until it was stiff. She moaned, and he pushed aside her hair and nuzzled the back of her neck.

"You're cold," she complained, and he pinched her nipple in response.

She jerked, her back arching, and he rubbed his stiff cock between her ass cheeks.

"Warm me up," he said.

She turned in his embrace and snuggled into him before kissing his thick neck. He groaned at the feel of her wet tongue licking his collarbone and threaded his fingers through her hair as she kissed across his chest. She stopped at one flat nipple and licked it experimentally. His breath hissed out, and he grunted when she nipped it.

"Minx," he whispered, and she smiled at him before soothing the sting with her tongue.

He shifted to his back, and she leaned over him eagerly, tasting his skin as she trailed her fingers up and down his ribs. When her mouth moved lower to just below his navel, he groaned again and used her hair to tug her head up.

"You need to stop, my sweet," he rasped.

"Why?" she asked. "I want to taste you. Please, can I?"

Her innocent request set his blood on fire. He hesitated, torn between conflicting emotions. He shouldn't let her suck his cock. He shouldn't teach her how to please him with her mouth and her tongue. Her future husband would know immediately of her lack of innocence if he did, but the thought of being in her mouth was a temptation he couldn't resist. He stared at her lips, imagined them stretched around his thick length, and relaxed his grip on her hair.

"Yes," he said.

"Thank you, Caleb." She gave him a shy smile that made his hand tighten again, and he pushed her head almost roughly toward his cock.

He groaned when he felt her warm breath on the head of

his cock. She gave him another shy look. "Do I… should I just start sucking?"

He kneaded her scalp before saying hoarsely, "Lick me first."

"Will you tell me if I'm not doing it right?"

"Yes," he said quickly.

The first tentative swipe of her tongue made his hips thrust, and a moan burst from his lips. She hesitated and then licked him again, tasting his entire cock with her warm wet tongue as he fisted the sheets and tried to keep control.

"Am I – is this right, Caleb?"

"Suck, Ellie," he gasped.

She slid him into her mouth, sucking experimentally on the head before tracing the ridge with her tongue.

"Ellie!" His breath exploded in a hot rush and he was helpless to stop from curling his hands into her hair.

He pushed gently, encouraging her to take more. She obliged eagerly, sliding her mouth halfway down his cock until he was resting against the back of her throat. She sucked gently, and he squeezed her head.

"Harder," he muttered.

She tightened her mouth around his cock, and he watched as her soft lips stretched up and down his throbbing cock.

When she tried to stop, he shook his head. "No, keep going. You don't stop until I tell you to, my sweet."

She continued to suck at his cock, little noises of pleasure escaping around his length as he thrust his hips against her mouth in a steady rhythm.

"Look at me," he ordered.

She raised her gaze obediently, and he smoothed her long dark hair back from her face. "You're doing so well," he praised. She flushed before sucking him with renewed vigour. His balls were tightening, and the tension in his belly was more than he could stand. With a muttered curse, he pulled her from his cock and watched with satisfaction when she licked his precum from her lips.

"Caleb? Did I - "

"Straddle me," he said.

She immediately climbed onto him, parting her thighs around his hips, and made a soft noise when his cock brushed against her pussy.

"Did you like that, Ellie? Did you like sucking my cock?" he asked.

"Yes," she said shyly. "I – I liked the noises you made when I was…"

She trailed off, and he reached up to cup her breasts, giving them a hard squeeze. "When you were sucking my cock. Say it, sweetheart."

"When I was sucking your cock," she whispered as her cheeks flamed a bright red.

"Good girl." He gave her a pleased look, and her fingers wrapped around his wrist when he dropped one hand between her thighs and cupped her pussy.

She was soaking wet, and he breathed a sigh of relief. She had enjoyed it. Just thinking about being in her mouth again made his cock twitch. He would spend the next few times allowing her to adjust to sucking him before he came in her mouth. Picturing her swallow every ounce of his seed made him want to come.

What next time? The blizzard is slowing, remember? There was a noticeable difference this morning, and it will most likely end today. By this time tomorrow, Ellie will be back with her father, and you'll be left with nothing but your hand and memories of her.

He shoved the thought away as Ellie moaned loudly. "Caleb, please touch me."

"I am touching you, sweetheart."

"No, move your fingers," she begged.

He grinned at her and rubbed her swollen button with the pads of his fingertips. She cried out and ground her pelvis against his hand, her nails digging into his wrists with almost painful intensity.

"Caleb, I need it!" she said in frustration, and he grinned again.

"Need what, sweetheart?"

"You know what!" she panted.

"I want you to say it," he said. "Tell me exactly what you need."

"I need your cock," she said quickly, and he rewarded her obedience by rubbing her clit firmly. God, her lack of inhibition and the way she totally gave in to the experience and the sensations made him harder than a rock. She had no idea how incredible she was in bed.

Yes, she'll make another man a fine wife and bed partner.

His stomach clenched at the thought of Ellie in another man's bed, and he sat up quickly, nearly dumping her from his lap.

She squealed in surprise and grabbed his shoulders as he slid his arm around her waist and gripped her tightly.

"Do you like my cock?" he asked.

She nodded. "Yes. I want it."

He dipped his head and nipped her earlobe, his hands stroking the smoothness of her back. "It's only my cock that you want. No other. Say it."

"I – it's only your cock that I want," she said breathlessly. Her voice had uncertainty, but it was overshadowed by her obvious eagerness to play this unexpected game.

He sucked on her earlobe before tracing the curve of her ear with his tongue. "That's right, sweet Ellie. It's only my cock that fucks your tight pussy."

"Yes," she agreed quickly. His cock was pressed against her core, and she rubbed against it. "Yes, Caleb."

He tugged her head back and kissed her until she was moaning and thrusting her pelvis against him wantonly.

"Not good enough," he whispered against her mouth. "Say it again."

"I," she licked her lips and dropped her gaze before murmuring, "It's only your cock that…"

She stopped, and he bit her bottom lip. "Say it."

"Caleb, I can't say that word."

"Why not?"

"Because it's coarse, and a gentleman doesn't want to hear a lady speak that way," she said.

He concealed his grin. He had been inside of Ellie, tasted her pussy, slid his cock into her warm mouth and watched as she sucked, and he found her refusal to say 'fuck' after all of that to be utterly charming.

"Perhaps now is the time to tell you I'm not a gentleman," he said.

"Yes, you are," she objected. "You're - "

He cut her off with a hard kiss, and she moaned happily when he stroked her clit with his fingers.

"I am not, sweet Ellie. I won't allow you to come until you say what I want to hear."

A stubborn look crossed her face, and he nearly laughed out loud. He was enjoying this hidden feisty side of Ellie. Without speaking, he increased the pressure of his fingers.

She clutched at his shoulders, her head falling back as he brought her closer and closer to the edge. When her body tensed, he stopped touching her, and she cried out in dismay and pounded on his back with her tiny fists.

"Tell me what I want to hear," he said.

"I will not," she declared breathlessly. "I am a lady, and I won't – oh!"

He had resumed his gentle touch against her clit, and she squirmed and moaned until he stopped again.

"Caleb!"

"Tell me," he whispered persuasively before dipping his head to suck on one tight nipple as he lightly and teasingly brushed her clit.

"Please, Caleb," she pleaded, and he bit her nipple lightly before shaking his head.

"Damn you!" She cursed before pounding his back again. He barely felt the blows, and he grinned at her.

"Punching me won't help, sweetheart."

He pinched her clit, and she shrieked breathlessly as her body arched against his.

"Oh please, oh please," she moaned.

"Say it." He nibbled the line of her jaw before tasting her with his tongue. "Say it, Ellie."

"Please fuck me," she whispered. "Please fuck my pussy."

"Again," he said.

"Please fuck me."

"Louder."

"Please fuck me!" she shouted.

In one smooth motion, he lifted her and thrust his cock deep into her waiting warmth. She sank down on him, her knees pressing against his thighs and her body shaking, and he cupped her face before kissing her lightly.

"Only my cock in your tight pussy, sweetheart."

"Only your cock," she agreed immediately and then squealed with delight when he made two hard, deep thrusts.

He was secretly delighted when she braced her hands on his shoulders and rode him. He leaned back so he could watch her pussy slide up and down his cock before lightly pressing against her clit with his fingers.

"Oh!" She stopped her up-and-down motion and switched to rocking against his fingertips.

He pressed his free hand between her magnificent

breasts, stopping her rocking motion, and she pouted adorably at him.

"Caleb, no."

"Keep fucking me."

"I am," she replied.

"No, you're trying to make yourself come."

She flushed, and he tweaked her nipple. "Fuck me, Ellie."

She bit her bottom lip before rising up and down on his cock. He groaned and watched her full breasts bounce before rubbing at her clit again.

She moaned loudly, and he gave her a pleased smile when she continued to fuck him.

"That's my good girl, sweetheart. Do you like fucking me?"

"Yes. Yes, I like fucking you," she said without hesitating. He tugged lightly at her clit before leaning forward again and wrapping his arm around her.

"I like fucking you too," he muttered into her ear. Holding her firmly, he plunged his cock in and out of her wet pussy.

She cried out, her hands sliding around his back and her nails digging shallow marks into his naked back. The slight pain only increased his desire, and he thrust rapidly in and out as he pinched and tugged at her swollen clit.

Her entire body tensing, she screamed and came all over his cock. The surge of wetness and the added pressure as her pussy squeezed him tightly in the throes of her orgasm pulled his climax from him, and he thrust one final time as his seed spilled into her.

She collapsed against him, panting harshly against his throat as he rubbed her damp back and kissed her pale shoulder.

"Oh, Caleb," she whispered. "That was so good."

"Mmm," he agreed against her shoulder before easing her off him and onto her side. She closed her eyes and tucked her body into a little ball as he curled around her. She burrowed her back and bottom into him, and he palmed her breast, running his fingers over her still-hard nipple before giving it a gentle squeeze.

"Are you hungry?" she murmured. "I can make you breakfast."

"No. Sleep, Ellie," he said.

* * *

ELLIE DRESSED SLOWLY, TRYING NOT TO WINCE. HER THIGHS ached, and there was a soreness between her legs that –

Pussy. Your pussy is sore, Ellie because Caleb fucked you so many times with his cock.

She blushed furiously and stared furtively at the bedroom door as if Caleb might hear her unladylike thoughts from the kitchen. It was close to dinner time, and they had spent most of the day together in bed. He had allowed her to nap for an hour before taking her again. This time, he hadn't teased or tormented. He'd simply rubbed her clit and sucked her nipples until she was moaning uncontrollably before spreading her thighs and fucking her. When her stomach began to growl close to noon, Caleb had gone to the kitchen and brought food to the bedroom. She had eaten more than she normally did - apparently, sex burned much of her energy - and Caleb had taken her again before she'd fallen asleep.

She touched her swollen mouth. Caleb had woken her in the most pleasant of ways. His tongue brushing against her clit as he stroked her hips and her thighs had brought her to climax twice. When she'd finally stopped moaning and shuddering, he'd stood next to the bed and tugged her to her knees. She had sucked at his cock willingly – her face burned at the memory of just how willing she'd been – and he had petted her hair and praised her softly as she did so. She hoped she was good at it, hoped she had pleased him. She liked the way he looked as he watched her take him in her mouth. Liked the way his eyes darkened and his face flushed with need.

What does it matter if he thinks you're good at it? The blizzard is over, and you'll return to your bed tonight. Your cold and lonely bed.

She blinked back the sudden tears that were threatening. The blizzard wouldn't last forever. She knew that, so why was she so upset? She should be happy. She had gotten what she wanted from Caleb and used him as she needed to, so there was no need to continue with him. Her innocence was gone, and Frederick would no longer want her.

I'll say your innocence is gone. When I told you to use Caleb, I didn't mean repeatedly.

Be quiet, she hissed at her inner voice.

Are you not the least bit ashamed? What will you do on your wedding night? You've only made it more difficult on yourself. Not only will you have to pretend it hurts, you'll have to pretend you have never sucked a cock, never had your pussy eaten, never –

Enough!

What happens if you cannot fool your future husband? What then?

It does not matter. I would prefer to remain a spinster forever.

Her inner voice had nothing to say about that, and she rubbed her forehead wearily. It was true, she realized sadly. She would rather remain a spinster forever than lie to a future husband.

Her inner voice didn't remain quiet for long. *No, you'll choose to be a spinster because you know that no one else will ever make you feel the way Caleb does.*

Perhaps if she asked him nicely, he would allow her to stay with him. He had made it clear that he didn't want her as a wife, but she was more than certain that she satisfied him in bed. She could think of worse things than cooking Caleb's meals and warming his bed.

Have you gone mad? You would live with a man who is not your husband and does not wish to be? Where is your self-respect? What happens when he decides to find a wife? A man like him will not be happy living a life alone forever. He has already pointed out that you are not sturdy or strong enough to be a farmer's wife. You may please him in bed, but eventually, you will find yourself tossed from his home when he goes in search of a wife.

Her inner voice was right. What she wanted was madness. She shook her head and walked to the bedroom door. She had lingered long enough. Caleb would be anxious to take her home.

He stood at one of the windows, staring at the setting sun, and she cleared her throat nervously. He didn't turn, and she crossed the room to tap him lightly on the back.

"Caleb? The blizzard is over."

She sounded extraordinarily stupid, even to herself, but Caleb simply nodded. She swallowed down her sudden anxiety. He had changed his mind about escorting her home. She didn't blame him, nor would she beg him to go with her. It would be hard on his horses and a cold journey for him, and her safety was not his problem.

"How far are you from town?" she asked.

"About two hours," he said.

She hid her dismay. Two hours by horse would be at least a six hour walk for her, probably more because of the deep snow. She squared her shoulders before taking her coat from the hook on the wall. She needed to leave now – it would be dark soon, and the more time she had to walk in the light, the better.

She buttoned her jacket and put on her gloves and hat before tapping Caleb on the back again. "Caleb? Thank you so much for your kindness. You saved my life, and I will forever be in your debt."

He nodded again, and she licked her lips nervously. She wanted to tell him how much she had enjoyed being in his bed. She wanted to thank him for being so gentle with her, but she was embarrassed and couldn't even imagine how she would say it.

Instead, she said, "Will you tell me which direction is town?"

He finally turned, scowling when he saw she was wearing her jacket. "What are you doing?"

"I have imposed on your kindness long enough. The blizzard is over, and I need to return home. My father will be worried about me."

"Will he?" he asked sullenly.

She blinked in surprise before nodding. "Of course he will."

He stared grimly at her, and she smiled hesitantly. "Thank you again. I enjoyed our time together. Perhaps the next time you are in town, you will visit me? I would like it if you did."

He made an unintelligible grunt. He stared at her almost angrily, and she nervously stepped toward the door. "I must get going. It will be dark soon, and the less time I walk in the dark, the better. Will you point me in the right direction?"

He grabbed her arm and scowled at her. "You are not walking to town, Ellie. Do not be so foolish."

She flushed miserably. "You have already done enough for me. I cannot expect you to put yourself in harm's way to deliver me home."

His hand tightened on her arm before he dropped it abruptly. "I will take you into town."

"Thank you," she replied. She supposed she should argue further, but truthfully, the thought of walking into town alone in the cold and the dark terrified her.

"Would you like me to make a quick supper before we leave?" she asked.

He shook his head. "It is too late to make the journey today. We will leave first thing in the morning."

An overwhelming sensation of relief overtook her. She would have another night with Caleb. Another night to feel his arms around her and to hear him say her name in his raspy voice.

"Is that a problem?" he asked gruffly.

"No," she said quickly, her voice trembling a little. "Tomorrow is fine. I would prefer it."

Perhaps she would get lucky, and another blizzard would start in the night.

She removed her outerwear and hung them on the hook before moving to the kitchen. "Are you hungry?"

"A little."

"Me too. I'll make us some dinner."

"Thank you," he said. "I'm going out to do the chores. Stay in the house, Ellie."

"I will," she said. "Thank you again, Caleb."

He nodded and shrugged into his jacket before leaving the house with Scout.

* * *

"You're sore."

Ellie looked up from her dinner plate. "I'm sorry?"

"You wince every time you stand and sit. You're sore," Caleb said.

"A little, yes."

"I was too rough with you." A note of anxiety in his voice made her rush to reassure him.

"No, I liked everything you did to me. I think it's just

75

because it was – that is, I am not used to that particular activity."

He scraped back his chair and tossed his remaining supper into Scout's food dish. She watched as he filled metal buckets with snow and placed them on top of the woodstove before bringing in the tub.

"Caleb," she said. "You do not have to - "

"Hush, Ellie," he said quietly.

He made her sit as he cleared the table and washed and dried the dishes. By the time he was finished, the buckets of snow had melted and bubbled gently. He poured them into the tub before holding his hand out to her.

She stood, trying not to wince and failing, before walking slowly to him. He unbuttoned her bodice and her skirt, making a low noise of displeasure at the layer of petticoats before removing each of them. When she was standing in only her chemise, he stroked her bare arms before reaching for the hem of it.

"Caleb," she said.

"I have seen you naked," he said gruffly. "There is no point in modesty."

"I know," she said. "I wanted to ask if you would join me in the tub."

He hesitated. "It's a small tub."

"It is," she acknowledged.

She unbuttoned his shirt when he hesitated and tugged it from his upper body. She traced her fingers across her chest, smiling slightly at his sharp inhale. He took a step back.

"I will bathe with you but won't take you again. You are too sore and need time to heal."

"I am not that sore," she said.

"Do not lie to me," he said sternly.

She tried to keep the pout from her face as he finished undressing before removing her chemise. His gaze travelled over her naked body, and she was more than pleased when his cock hardened.

"Get into the tub," he said hoarsely.

She climbed in carefully, scooting to the front so he could climb in behind her. When he was seated, she leaned against his chest. She let her ass brush against his erection and smiled when he groaned under his breath.

"Behave, Ellie,"

"I am," she said sweetly.

"You are not," he growled.

To her dismay, despite the way she tried to entice him by taking her time in washing, he remained unaffected. Well, not entirely unaffected. His cock still rubbed against her ass and lower back, and there was a rather pained look on his face when he dipped his hand below the water's surface and cleaned it. But he only touched her as much as necessary, and as soon as they were clean, he stood and pulled her to her feet. She dried off quickly but was shivering by the time she was done. She shook her head when he held out her chemise.

"No, I would prefer to keep it clean for tomorrow's travels."

"What will you wear to bed?" he said.

"Do I need to wear something?" she asked innocently. "There are plenty of blankets, and if I get too cold, you will warm me."

"Ellie," he said warningly, "I already told you that I would not -"

"I'm cold. Let's go to bed."

"It's early," he said.

She shrugged, feeling bold, needy, and uncertain all at the same time. She dropped the towel at her feet and walked slowly toward the bedroom. "I'm tired. Good night."

He cursed under his breath, and a secret smile crossed her lips when she heard his footsteps behind her. Without looking at him, she climbed into the bed, waited as he blew out the candle, and climbed in beside her.

She shivered delicately, and when he made no move to pull her closer, she slid across the bed and nestled her body against his.

"Warm me, Caleb."

He groaned softly but put his arm around her, rubbing her back and upper arm as she reached down and grasped his cock. She stroked it slowly, running her thumb over the top as he moaned harshly.

"We can't. You're too sore."

"I will have plenty of time to heal after tonight," she said. "I want you to fuck me."

He inhaled, his hand squeezing compulsively around her arm as she smiled sweetly at him. "Will you deny me?"

"No," he said hoarsely. "No, my sweet Ellie."

She tilted her head and kissed him softly. He deepened it immediately, rolling her onto her back and pushing her thighs apart so that he could rest between them. She loved the feel of his body on her, loved the heavy weight of him, and she closed her eyes and tried to memorize the way it felt.

"Open your eyes," he demanded.

She obeyed, staring up at him as he reached between them and stroked her clit. She was already wet, and he made a low noise of satisfaction before slowly easing his cock into her wet, tight entrance.

She kept any evidence of the slight pain from her face and rubbed his back encouragingly. "Yes, Caleb. Yes."

He pushed lightly in and out, studying her face anxiously in the darkness. She stroked his cheek soothingly. "It does not hurt."

She wasn't lying. The slight edge of pain had already dulled, and the familiar tingle of pleasure was building in her lower body. She spread her legs wide and braced her feet on the bed as he propped himself on his hands above her. He started a slow slide and retreat motion, making heat pool in her center. She caressed his skin as he deftly stroked her until she was breathing raggedly and begging him to move faster.

He refused, keeping up the same unrelenting and torturous pace as she moved restlessly beneath him. She met each of his strokes with a quick upward thrust of her hips and smiled with satisfaction when it escalated his pace.

Before long, he was driving her into the mattress over and over again, and each thick slide of his cock practically liquefied her insides. She cried his name as he pushed her to the edge of her climax and then shoved her over. He moaned her name before kissing her with fierce possessiveness. He groaned loudly as he came - she felt the reverberation of it in his ribcage - and trembled madly before collapsing against her softness.

Her legs shaking from the force of her orgasm, she stroked his back and murmured soothing words of comfort into his ear as he buried his face in her neck. He stayed inside of her long after he had softened. When he finally eased away, a fleeting sense of loss and sorrow went through her, and she blinked back the sudden tears.

"What's wrong?" he asked worriedly. "Did I hurt you?"

"No," she said. "You didn't hurt me. Please, will you hold me?"

He nodded, and she curled into his hard, warm body and clung tightly to him.

CHAPTER 6

"It's not much longer now," Caleb said moodily.

Ellie nodded and tried to smile cheerfully at him. She was freezing despite the blanket Caleb had wrapped around her before leaving his farm. She wished longingly to be back in his home and his warm bed.

It was too late for that. They had woken early in the morning to clear skies and bright sunlight, and after a quick breakfast, Caleb saddled the horses and boosted her onto one.

"The snow is too deep for the wagon," he had explained.

She shifted on the horse and patted its warm neck when it neighed softly before staring at Caleb's broad back. The snowdrifts were deep, and he had kept a slow and steady pace for their horses.

He glanced back at her. "Are you all right?"

"Yes, I'm fine," she said. "Are you?"

"Why wouldn't I be?"

"You're very quiet."

He shrugged and turned away. After another fifteen

minutes of riding, she could see the edge of town. Her heart pounded in her chest, and she took a few deep breaths as they rode through main street. She could see her father's home, and she was suddenly anxious to see her father, despite how her stomach rolled with nausea at the thought of leaving Caleb. He would be so happy to see her alive.

"It is the last house on the right," she called to Caleb.

"I know," he said shortly.

She frowned at his tone but didn't say anything as they stopped in front of her home. Caleb swung out of the saddle and tied his horse to the post before lifting her down and tying her horse next to his. His hands lingered on her waist, and she smiled up at him.

"You must meet my father."

A strange look flickered over his face, and he shook his head. "No."

"Oh, but you must," she said. "He will want to meet the man who saved my life. Please, Caleb. For me?"

Before he could answer, she pulled him toward the front door.

"Ellie, I need to pick up some supplies and return home. I cannot - "

"Please," she pleaded as she opened the front door. "You can't leave without meeting Father."

"Ellie?" Her father's voice was loud and filled with surprise, and she felt Caleb flinch behind her.

"Caleb? What's wrong?"

He was white as a ghost and looked like he would vomit.

"Caleb? Are you ill? Do you need to sit down?"

"Ellie!" She was yanked from Caleb's grasp, and she laughed happily and hugged her father.

"You're alive!" He pulled back and stared anxiously at her before hugging her again. "Oh, my child, I was so worried. How did you survive?"

"I stumbled onto Caleb's farm, and he helped me. He saved my life, Father. You must meet him."

She turned and smiled encouragingly at Caleb. "Caleb, this is my father, Abraham Walters. Father, this is Caleb Thornwell."

* * *

CALEB STARED AT THE DOCTOR'S HAND WHEN HE STEPPED forward and held it out. "It's nice to meet you. Thank you for helping my baby girl."

He didn't take the doctor's hand. Ellie gave him a puzzled look, and Caleb stepped back as her father frowned at him. He could feel his body beginning to shake, could feel the rage from those first few horrible weeks after Missy's death returning. He stared at Ellie's father as the man frowned again.

"Is he mute, Ellie?"

"No, Father. Caleb, are you feeling ill?"

"You don't remember me," Caleb said. "Do you?"

"I'm sorry?" Abraham looked him up and down. "Have we met before?"

Caleb barked harsh laughter, and Ellie jumped when he slammed his hand against the wall. "Two years ago, I stood in this very hallway and begged you to help my dying wife. I begged you for help, and you refused because I didn't have the money to pay you. My wife and our unborn child died in the street outside of this house because you're a greedy, sorry excuse for a human being."

"Oh, Caleb," Ellie whispered before giving her father a horrified look. "Father, how could you?"

"Be quiet, girl," her father snapped before glaring at Caleb. "I am grateful to you for saving my daughter's life, but you need to leave."

"I did more than just save her life," Caleb said in a low voice. "I vowed to take my revenge for the deaths of my wife and daughter, and, after all this time, I have."

"What the hell are you talking about?" Abraham said warily. "Listen, I have to run a business. If I helped every poor farmer who came knocking on my door in the middle of the night, I would - "

"Her innocence," Caleb said. "I took your daughter's innocence."

He took a step forward, ignoring Ellie's gasp of dismay as her father's face whitened.

"She begged me to take it, pleaded for me - a poor, stupid farmer - to take her to my bed. How does that make you feel? Knowing that your beloved daughter's virginity was mine to take? Knowing that I repeatedly took what she offered freely to me?"

"Caleb, stop," Ellie moaned.

The red-hot rage surrounding him lifted slightly, and he glanced at Ellie. Her face was the colour of a sheet, and her eyes were huge. Her look of betrayal shamed him to his very core. What had he done?

"Get out!" her father suddenly shouted. "Get out!"

"Gladly," Caleb said. Forcing himself not to look at Ellie one last time, he turned and left. The door slammed behind him, and he quickly untied the horses before mounting his horse and riding down the street, leading the second behind him.

Do you feel better, my darling? Was the look on her father's face worth the hurt you bestowed on that sweet girl? She trusted you, she might have even loved you a little, and you took the gift she willingly gave you and twisted it into something ugly. Was it worth it?

Get out of my head, Missy, he snarled inwardly and rode forward blindly as his stomach rolled with nausea.

* * *

"Father," Ellie whispered. "Father, I can explain."

"Is it true? Did you give that – that *farmer* your virginity?" He asked in a quiet voice.

"Yes," she said. "It's true."

"How could you?" He whispered before glancing at the open doorway of the parlour. "Frederick – it was Frederick's to take, not his."

"Frederick tried to violate me. I almost died because of him. He attacked me, and I was forced to run away in a blizzard to escape him."

"Frederick would not do such a thing," Abraham said. "He is a good man."

"He did," Ellie insisted. "Why would I lie about this?"

"Because you are a silly little girl with her head in the clouds!" He suddenly hissed at her. "You have no idea what you've done."

His mouth trembled, and he swallowed compulsively before glancing at the parlour again. "Perhaps there is a way to salvage this. Perhaps - "

"Father," Ellie said loudly, "I will not marry Frederick. He tried to violate me."

"As if he would have you now!" her father shouted. "Do you honestly believe a respectable man like Frederick Barns would want a common whore?"

"Father," Ellie whispered before shrinking back. "Please, I know you are disappointed in me for sleeping with Caleb, but I had no choice. Frederick wanted me because of my virginity. It was a – a prize to him. I knew the only way to escape him was by giving it to another."

"Of course that's what he wanted! It's all you're good for, you stupid fool!" Her father roared. "And you had to ruin everything because you couldn't keep your legs closed to the first man who asked you to open them!"

"That isn't true!" Ellie cried before taking his arm. "If you would listen to me, you would see why I - "

"Get out," her father whispered before slumping against the wall. "Get out of my home, Ellie."

"Father?" Ellie said as fear clutched at her heart. "Father, this is my home too."

"No, it isn't. Leave and never come back."

"I am your child," Ellie said in disbelief. She tried to take his arm again and cried out when her father shoved her toward the door.

"I said get out! I never want to see you again. Do you understand?"

"I have no place to go," she whispered.

"Find your poor farmer," he snarled. "Perhaps if you get down on your knees and beg, if you offer to let him fuck you again, he will take pity on you."

"Father, please - "

"GET OUT!" he screamed, and she flinched back at the look of pure rage on his face before stumbling out of the house.

* * *

ABRAHAM SLAMMED THE DOOR BEHIND HIS DAUGHTER AND locked it before placing a trembling hand over his eyes. He jerked when the voice spoke from the parlour.

"Well, this is unfortunate. Isn't it, Abraham?"

"Frederick," Abraham said. "I can fix this. My daughter is still - "

"Your daughter," Frederick said, "has been soiled by that disgusting farmer. She is no longer of any use to me, which means I'll be requiring full payment of that loan after all, Dr. Walters."

"We can work something else out," Abraham said. "She was only gone for a few days. There could still be many ways she is innocent."

Frederick snorted loudly before pulling on his gloves. "The girl is damaged merchandise. I might as well go to the saloon and fuck one of Millie's girls. You have a month to repay the loan."

He swept out of the house, and Abraham sank to the floor before burying his head in his hands.

* * *

"ELLIE? OH MY GOODNESS, ELLIE! YOU'RE ALIVE! I WAS SO worried about you. The whole town thought you were dead after you got lost in the woods. You should never have wandered away from Frederick. Both he and your father were beside themselves with worry. How did you survive the blizzard?"

Ellie burst into tears as Louise stared in bewilderment. "My love, what is wrong?"

"Father has kicked me out," Ellie sobbed as Louise ushered her into the house.

"What do you mean he kicked you out?"

"I did something that disappointed him, and he became terribly angry. I've never seen him like that, Louise. He screamed at me and told me to leave his home and never come back."

"What? Why that doesn't make any sense. What could you have possibly done to make him kick you out of your home?" Louise hurried her into the kitchen and helped her out of her jacket and hat before pushing her gently into a kitchen chair.

Ellie, tears streaming down her face, stared around blurrily. "Where is your mother?"

"Out running a few errands," Louise said. She sat down beside Ellie and took her cold hands. "Ellie, I'm your best friend, and I love you. Please tell me what's wrong."

* * *

AN HOUR LATER, HER TEARS DRIED UP AND THE MUG OF TEA sitting untouched in front of her, Ellie glanced at Louise. "Do you believe me to be a whore?"

"Of course not," Louise said immediately. "Ellie, don't say that about yourself."

"My father thinks I am one," Ellie said dully.

"Your father is a fool."

"No, I am," Ellie said. "I thought I – I would use Caleb to escape Frederick. I felt guilty about it, but it turns out that he was only using me as well."

She laughed bitterly. "Yet, I still feel terrible about it."

"Honey, this Caleb isn't a good man."

"He is," Ellie insisted. "Louise, if you met him, you would see he is. I don't blame him for what he did. My father allowed his wife and baby to die because he was poor. I would also be angry and take my revenge however I could."

"That doesn't make it right. Caleb is no better than Frederick."

Ellie shook her head. "Don't say that. Caleb is – he *was* warm and kind and gentle to me. He worried about hurting me, and he – he made me feel good."

"He used you."

"Yes, and I used him. We both got what we wanted, did we not?"

"Oh, Ellie," Louise said. "I'm sorry, my love."

Ellie sighed. "Could I stay with you, Louise? I hate to impose, but I have nowhere else to go."

"Of course you can. Father and Mother love you and I know they will welcome you in their home for as long as you need. Do not worry. You're safe with us."

"Thank you, Louise. I owe you a great debt," Ellie said.

Louise squeezed her hand. "You do not."

The front door slammed, and Louise squeezed her hand again as a voice called, "Louise? Where are you?"

"In the kitchen, Mother."

"You will not believe what has happened! Ellie is alive!"

Louise smiled at Ellie. "Yes, I know, Mother. She is - "

"She stumbled onto a farm, and the man there, Caleb Farnswell or Thornwell perhaps– I'm not entirely sure as I've never met the man – saved her life. And do you know what your proper, well-bred friend did?"

Louise's mother hurried into the kitchen, dropping her bags on the counter before spinning to face the table. "She opened her legs like a little whore and let the man defile her in countless ways. Mrs. Millsworth told me that she let him…"

She trailed off, her mouth dropping open as she caught sight of Ellie. "Wh-what is she doing here?"

"Mother, Ellie is going to stay with us for a while. Her father has thrown her from her home, and she - "

"No, she is not," Louise's mother said firmly. "Leave, Ellie, right now."

"Mother!" Louise snapped. "What is wrong with you?"

"The girl is the talk of the town. Everyone already knows what she did with that farmer, and I will not have your reputation dragged down with hers. You are a respectable girl with a bright future who would not willingly sleep with a man she isn't married to. I forbid you to be friends with her."

"I'm twenty-two, Mother. Your days of forbidding me to do things are over."

"Not while you live under my roof!" Her mother shouted. She glared at Ellie. "Leave, Ellie. If you truly are my daughter's friend, you'll leave and never talk to her again. Do you want her to be gossiped about by the entire town?"

"Mrs. Handon," Ellie whispered. "I'm sorry, but how do you know what happened?"

Louise's mother snorted. "Nothing is a secret in this town for long, girl. Did you honestly think no one would find out that you allowed a man who was not your husband to soil you in such a manner? Now, leave. I will not ask you again."

"Mother! You cannot - "

"I can and I will! And if I don't, your father will!" she shouted. "Leave, Ellie!"

Ellie grabbed her jacket and hurried out of the house as Louise chased after her.

"Ellie, wait!"

"Get back in the house, Louise!" Her mother yanked her back inside and slammed the door shut.

Sobbing softly, Ellie staggered down the street. She ignored the curious looks of the people she passed by. Her stomach growled loudly despite her anxiety. She had eaten nothing since the cold breakfast with Caleb this morning, and it was past noon.

Get used to being hungry, girl. You have no money, remember?

Panic fluttered in her stomach, and she forced a few harsh breaths into her lungs. It was cold, and it would be dark in a few hours. If she didn't find a place to stay, she would freeze to death. She briefly considered returning to her father, pounding on the door and begging him to open it. But she thought again of the look on Caleb's face when he had spoken of his dead wife and child and recoiled at the thought of living with her father. Perhaps it was for the best that he had kicked her out. After what he had done to Caleb, she would never see her father in the same way again.

Think, Ellie. Think.

She could walk back to Caleb's farm. If she apologized for her father, if she offered to cook his meals and warm his bed, perhaps he would –

Don't be daft, girl. He slept with you because he wanted revenge against your father. He doesn't care for you – he never did.

Her shoulders slumped, and she buried her face in her hands. That was very true. She couldn't return to Caleb's. All that would happen is he would reject her, and she would freeze to death on the prairies rather than in town.

She wandered down the street, past the general store and the hotel. Across from the hotel, the saloon – its insides already lit up with bright light – caught her attention. She stared fixedly at it for a moment before crossing the street.

Ellie, you can't!

She could, and she would. She had no choice.

She shoved open the door and stepped timidly inside. She had never been in the saloon and swallowed nervously as a man sitting at the table closest to the door looked her up and down. He was big, with a bushy beard and dirty hands, and she ignored his look as one of the saloon girls plopped down on his lap. Her dress was scandalously low-cut, and he leaned forward and planted a wet kiss on her cleavage before squeezing her ass. She squealed and laughed and slapped him lightly on the chest.

The saloon was already half-full, and Ellie carefully weaved her way between the tables to the long curved bar. The bartender was wiping down the top with a piece of cloth, and he raised his eyebrows at her.

"Can I help you?"

"Yes, I," she licked her lips and smiled tentatively at him, "I was wondering if I could speak to you about employment."

"Employment," he said.

"Yes. I thought perhaps I could - "

"Millie!" the man suddenly shouted.

Ellie flinched and stepped back as a heavy-set woman, her ample curves poured into a dark green dress, and her red hair gleaming in the light materialized beside her. "What is it?"

"This girl's lookin' for work."

Millie looked her up and down, her painted lips parting to reveal yellow teeth. "The good doctor's daughter. Ellie, isn't it?"

"I'm sorry, have we met before?" Ellie asked.

Millie laughed and shook her head. "No. You and me – we don't exactly run in the same social circles, now do we? I ain't got time for knitting and embroidery."

Millie patted her arm. "But everyone in town knows the doctor's daughter."

She leaned a little closer and gave Ellie a scrutinizing look. "So sweet, so lovely and pure. Although," she paused and gave Ellie a little wink, "not as pure as you once were, I reckon."

Ellie flushed brightly, and Millie laughed again. "What's happened, my soiled dove? Has your father been shamed by his only child's transgressions with the farmer? Has he forced his little dove to fly from the nest?"

Ellie wanted to leave. She wanted to turn and escape the woman and this horrid place, but she took a deep breath and said, "I'm looking for employment. I," she glanced at the piano in the far corner of the saloon, "I have skill in playing the piano. Are you in need of a musician?"

With an odd little grin on her face, Millie shook her head. "We ain't."

Ellie's face fell, and her shoulders slumped. Playing piano

at the saloon was her only idea. "Very well, thank you for your time, Miss Millie."

She turned to leave, and Millie took her arm in a firm grip. "Hold on. We're not in need of a piano player, but there's employment to be found if you need it."

"Doing what?" Ellie whispered.

Millie smiled, and Ellie followed her gaze up the staircase. Dressed provocatively in stockings and her chemise, a woman with her lipstick smeared and her hair a dark messy cloud around her face was exiting one of the rooms above the saloon floor. A man followed her, buttoning his pants and shrugging into his jacket. Ellie watched as he kissed her and slapped her roughly on the ass before ambling down the staircase. The woman leaned against the railing and waved at another man sitting at a table. He nodded and finished his beer before starting up the stairs.

Ellie gave Millie a horrified look. "N-no, I can't do that."

"Why not?" Millie held her arm tightly and stepped forward until her face was only inches from Ellie's. "You know what it's like to have a man between those smooth thighs of yours. Your virginity is gone forever. What difference does it make who fucks you now?"

"B-because I can't, I mean, it isn't - "

Millie squeezed her arm until she gasped. "Your father has driven you from your home and you have no money and no place to go. Is that not right, my soiled dove?"

Mesmerized by Millie's dark stare, Ellie nodded.

"You will freeze to death. I can offer you a warm place, safety and money. All you have to do is part your legs and let a man do what comes naturally to him."

She stroked a strand of Ellie's dark hair. "You're so pretty and sweet looking. I guarantee you will be very popular. Why, you may only have to work for a year or so before you have enough money to return to the East. Then this, your life in the West, will be nothing more than a bad dream. You can start again, little dove. No one will ever have to know of your past."

Ellie stared silently at her, and Millie smiled again before leading her toward the staircase. "Come, child. You're cold and hungry. I have a hot bath and a good meal waiting for you. After, we will find you a pretty dress to wear. One that will be sure to please, hmm?"

Feeling numb and disconnected from her body, Ellie followed Millie up the stairs.

* * *

CALEB TIED HIS HORSES TO THE LONG WOODEN HITCHING POST outside the saloon. He had picked up his supplies and loaded them onto the second horse, and he should have been heading home. On his way into town with Ellie, he had stopped briefly at his friend Joseph's farm. Joseph was a bachelor, and when the weather was better, he often dropped by Caleb's place to visit. Caleb had asked the man to do his evening chores if he had not returned in time. Joseph had agreed cheerfully. Caleb knew Joseph would honour his promise but if he left now, he would make it home in time to not impose on Joseph.

So why aren't you leaving, my darling?

He didn't know why.

You do. You're staying because of Ellie. Go to her, my darling. Beg for her forgiveness.

He couldn't do that. The look on her face when he had told her father what they had done... she hated him, and he would never see her again. She was safe at home with her father, and she would find another man to marry and warm her at night. He would become nothing more than a distant memory to her.

He climbed the steps to the saloon and, once inside, ordered a beer from the bartender before finding an empty table. He sipped moodily at the beer as one of the saloon girls drifted toward him. He shook his head, and she gave him a disappointed pout before walking away.

Go home, Caleb. There's no point in hanging around town. Ellie is finished with you. You treated her horribly, and that shame you're feeling? It is never going to go away.

You could try, my darling, Missy's voice whispered. *Please return to Ellie's home and try.*

"Mr. Thornwell, is it?"

He looked up, his entire body stiffening as the man dropped into the empty chair across from him. "Do you mind if I join you? It's rather busy in here this evening."

"I do mind." Caleb gripped his mug of beer tightly as Frederick Barns grinned at him.

"Come now, Mr. Thornwell. There's no need for rudeness."

"If you don't leave right now, I'll - "

"Did you enjoy taking what was mine?" Frederick tugged lightly on the ends of his waxed mustache as Caleb glared at him.

"It wasn't yours."

"Oh, but it was," Frederick replied. "Her father had given her to me."

His voice a thick growl, Caleb said, "She's a grown woman. Her father could no more *give* her to you like some prized cow then - "

"Did you know our good doctor has a small problem with gambling?" Frederick said.

"I know nothing about the man," Caleb snapped.

"No, I suppose you don't," Frederick said thoughtfully. "He does, though. In fact, it isn't really a small problem but a large one. He came to me a few months ago, requiring help with a rather significant sum of money he owed to a nasty group of cowboys. Never play poker with cowboys, Mr. Thornwell," he advised, "they cheat."

"What's your goddamn point?" Caleb snarled.

"My point is that I loaned Dr. Walters the money he needed to keep those rough cowboys from killing him. Dr. Walters assured me, quite emphatically, that he would pay the money in full in less than a month, with interest, of course. Unfortunately, as it so often happens, he could not come up with the money. When he realized that I intended to announce to the entire town his gambling sins, he offered me his sweet and oh so lovely daughter as payment. The man's reputation is indescribably important to him. I've never seen anything like it."

"He what?" Caleb rasped. He felt like the floor had dropped out from under his feet, and he latched onto the table with both hands before leaning forward.

Frederick nodded. "I have a, shall we say, fondness for sweet, young virginal girls, so you can imagine that I was more than agreeable to his new terms of payment. I even agreed to court the child and promised her father I would marry her before taking her virtue. It was a lie, of course. I have no wish to be saddled with a wife, but when I spoke to Abraham about taking Ellie riding unaccompanied, he was more than willing to allow it. I finally had my chance to take what belonged to me. Unfortunately, the girl was more of a handful than I imagined. Do you know I required fifteen stitches? I was displeased, to say the least."

"Does he know what you tried to do?" Caleb said hoarsely.

"Sweet little Ellie told him, but he refused to believe it. Although just between us, I think he knows. In fact, I think he's known all along that I never intended to marry his precious daughter."

Frederick leaned forward and smiled at Caleb. "You believe me to be a monster, but Dr. Walters is the real monster. Don't you agree?"

"Does Ellie know?" Caleb asked. He rolled his hands into tight fists as Frederick laughed.

"Of course not. She's a sweet but simple girl who wouldn't believe it even if Abraham confessed. She adores her father. Or," he paused and gazed up to the second level of the saloon, "she used to."

Caleb followed his gaze. All of the breath escaped his lungs in a hard rush. He felt like he'd been punched in the gut, and he stared wide-eyed at Ellie as she walked slowly down the staircase. She wore a teal-coloured dress that fell to just below her knees. The bodice was cut so low that over half of her breasts were exposed. Her dark hair was piled high on her head, with tendrils of curls arranged artfully around her face. She wore dark shadow on her eyelids, rouge covered her cheeks, and her lips were painted a bright red.

"What is she doing here?" he said.

"Did you not hear?" Frederick said cheerfully. "Her father kicked her out with nothing more than the clothes on her back. The poor soiled dove has no place else to go."

Caleb swallowed heavily as Ellie, her face pale except for the colour painted high on her cheeks, stared fearfully at the man approaching her. She shrank back and a chubby woman appeared next to her before taking her arm and pulling her to the man. She smiled at the man and held Ellie's arm tightly as he looked her up and down.

"I suppose that's my fault," Frederick continued. "Why, I was so distraught over hearing that the woman I was courting - the woman I would marry - had allowed herself to be defiled by a common farmer like you that I simply could not keep it to myself. I usually abhor gossiping, but I'll confess that I found it rather enjoyable to spread the news of the good daughter's debasement."

When Caleb didn't reply - his gaze was still glued to the visibly trembling Ellie - Frederick cleared his throat loudly.

"It's a shame that someone as lovely as she is will soon spread her legs for any man who tosses a few bills her way. I plan on taking a turn this evening with the soiled dove before she becomes completely ruined. She was only with you for a few days. I'm certain you didn't take all of her," he paused and smiled at Caleb, "holes."

Frederick's eyes widened when Caleb reached across and grabbed him by the jacket. Caleb threw him onto the table before punching him repeatedly in the face. Frederick screamed pitifully and tried to squirm away but was no match for Caleb's rage-fueled strength.

He punched the banker over and over, feeling his nose break beneath his pounding fist. Pain flared in his hand, but he ignored it grimly as he continued to hammer his fist into Frederick's face.

"I will kill you if you touch her. Do you hear me?" he snarled.

Frederick was a limp ragdoll, and Caleb shook him roughly before punching him again. "Do you hear me?"

"Caleb! Stop!"

He stopped with his fist drawn back, one hand holding Frederick around the throat and blood dripping steadily onto the floor. Panting harshly, he stared at Ellie as she touched his arm timidly.

"Please stop," she said softly.

He dropped Frederick to the table with a harsh thud. The man groaned softly, and Caleb yanked off his jacket before bundling Ellie into it and buttoning it to her throat, covering her pale skin from the other men's gazes. He took her hand and pulled her toward the door.

"What are you doing?" Ellie said in confusion.

"Hey! Where are you taking her?" The chubby woman grabbed his arm and dropped it immediately when Caleb turned his gaze to her.

"She – she works for me," the woman said tentatively.

"Leave!" Caleb snarled at her. The woman skittered away as Caleb led Ellie out of the saloon.

"Caleb," Ellie said, "Please, I can't - "

"Hush, Ellie," he snapped, and she stopped protesting when he lifted her onto his horse. He untied both horses before climbing into the saddle behind her. He rode toward her father's home. Ellie stiffened against him when he stopped in front of the house and slid off the horse.

"I can't go back here," she said.

He lifted her from his horse without speaking and carried her to the front door. He set her on her feet and pounded on the door with his uninjured hand.

"Caleb," Ellie said again, "my father has asked me to - "

The door swung open, and her father's eyes widened. "What are you doing here?"

Caleb shoved him back, and Ellie moaned quietly as her father stumbled and fell to the floor.

"Get your things, Ellie," Caleb said grimly.

"Wh-what?"

"Go to your room and get some clothing and whatever else you require," he repeated before pushing her gently down the hall. "Go quickly."

With a nervous look at her father, Ellie ran down the hall and disappeared up the staircase. Caleb crouched next to Abraham. The doctor moaned and shrank back when Caleb raised his scraped and bleeding hand and showed it to him.

"I know what you did," he said in a low voice. "I know how you sold your only daughter to a despicable man who tried to rape her. If you go near her again, if you try to contact her again, I'll break both of your hands."

Caleb leaned forward until his face was inches from Abraham's. "It's hard to be a doctor without the use of your hands. Do you agree?"

The man nodded and closed his eyes as Caleb poked him lightly in the chest. "Stay away from her. Do you understand?"

"Y-yes," the doctor whispered.

Caleb grunted with satisfaction before straightening. Ignoring the man cowering on the floor at his feet, he waited patiently for Ellie to return.

CHAPTER 7

Ellie finished scrubbing her face before adding fresh water to the basin and rinsing away the soap. It was a cold journey from town to Caleb's farm, and Caleb hadn't spoken a word during the entire trip.

When they finally arrived, he carried her into the house before bringing in the bag she had packed and the supplies he had bought. He had given her a terse command to stay in the house before taking the horses to the barn.

She removed the horrible clothing that Millie had dressed her in and pulled out a simple shirt and skirt. She hadn't packed very much – she was worried that Caleb would do something to her father if she lingered too long – and she hesitated before repacking her bag. Her fingers traced the picture of her mother she had stuffed into the bag. She stared fixedly at it before closing the bag and setting it on the floor of the spare bedroom.

The dress, corset, and petticoats Millie had given her were crumpled on the floor. She was tempted to throw them into the fire, but instead, she picked them up and draped them across the sofa. She was thankful that Caleb had given her a place to stay for the night, but by tomorrow, she would be back at the saloon. She had nowhere else to go, and she was deeply ashamed to admit that to Caleb. She felt incredibly stupid for being so blind to her father's true nature. Once Caleb found out her father refused to allow her back into the house, she would be even more ashamed.

She sighed and sat down at the table before dropping her head into her hands. What did it matter what Caleb thought of her? They had used each other for their own gain, and that was it. She shouldn't have allowed him to take her away, but the thought of those men in the saloon touching her had frightened her badly. She wiped at the tears that were sliding down her cheeks. It didn't matter how frightened she was. She needed to accept that she had no choice. She would walk back into town tomorrow and ask Millie to hire her again. Hopefully, she would have enough money to return to the East in a year or so. Her mother's sister would take her in. She was certain of it.

The door opened, and Caleb and Scout entered in a rush of cold air that took her breath away. Scout barked happily and bounded across the room to lick at her hands. She petted him gently as Caleb removed his jacket and boots and sat across from her.

"Ellie?" he said gently. "Are you okay?"

She nodded. A curious numbness had settled over her, and she stared woodenly at him before struggling to her feet.

"I'll make you dinner."

"No," he said. "I don't need dinner. Sit down and rest, and I'll make you something to eat."

"I'm not hungry," she said, returning to her seat.

"You have to eat."

She shook her head. "I've already been a burden for you. I have no money to pay you for food, and I refuse to take advantage of your generosity any longer."

"Ellie, I - "

She suddenly laughed bitterly. "That's not entirely true, is it? After all, I am back in your home and looking forward to having a warm place to sleep for the night."

"Ellie, please listen to me," Caleb pleaded. "I am so sorry for using you the way I did. It was horrible of me to do so, and I am truly ashamed of my behaviour. I wish I had never - "

"It's fine," she interrupted dully. "I used you as well."

"What do you mean?"

She forced her gaze to his. "I seduced you into taking my virginity so that I would not have to marry Frederick. You were right, you know. I knew my father would take Frederick's word over mine, so I hatched a plan to seduce you so that I would no longer be a virgin. It was the only thing Frederick wanted from me."

"You didn't seduce me. I seduced you."

"Does it matter in the end, Caleb?" she asked. "We both got what we wanted."

He gave her a sick look, and she shook her head wearily. "I am not angry with you. What my father did was terrible, and I do not blame you for using me to get back at him. I would have done the same if I were in your place."

"No, you wouldn't have," he said angrily. "You're a good person. You're sweet and thoughtful and - "

"That's kind of you to say, but we both know it isn't true. I used you for my gain and didn't care that it might hurt or upset you. Frankly, I was glad to hear you had your own motives for sleeping with me. It makes my guilt a little easier to bear."

He reached for her hand and she pushed back her chair and stood up. "If you don't mind, I think I will go to bed. It's late, and I have a long journey tomorrow."

"Journey? Ellie, what do you mean?" he said, but she had already walked to the spare bedroom and opened the door.

"Good night, Caleb."

She disappeared into the room and shut the door firmly behind her.

* * *

THE NEXT MORNING, HE WOKE FROM A FITFUL DOZE TO THE smell of cooked meat. He dressed quickly, wincing at the pain in his swollen hand before hurrying into the kitchen. A plate of food was warming on top of the wood stove, and he scowled at Ellie as she buttoned her jacket before throwing her bag over her shoulder. The clothing she wore last night was draped across the sofa, and she picked them up and folded them neatly over her arm before smiling at him.

"I made you breakfast as a token of my appreciation for giving me a place to stay the night. Thank you again, Caleb. Goodbye."

He rushed over and grabbed her arm. "Where do you think you're going?"

"To town," she said.

"Back to your father?" he asked angrily.

A look of embarrassment crossed her face before she straightened her back and said, "No. My father has asked me to leave his home. I shamed him greatly with my behaviour, and he said he would prefer it if I found another place to live."

"I know that," he said.

"How do you know?" she asked.

"You're going back to the saloon, aren't you?" He stared at the clothing in her arms.

"Yes," she said. "I thought I would stay with my friend Louise's family, but her mother was understandably upset when she learned of my...indiscretion and did not wish for her daughter's reputation to be as sullied as mine. Millie very kindly offered me employment, and I accepted."

"You are not going back there," Caleb snarled.

"I have no choice," she said. "I need both food and shelter and as part of my employment, I am allowed to stay in the rooms above the saloon."

"You're staying here," he said. He reached for the buttons on her jacket, and she batted his hand away.

"I can't," she said. "You've already been generous enough in sheltering me from the blizzard and - "

"You're not going back to that saloon!" he shouted, and she flinched away from him.

"I'm sorry, I didn't mean to yell," he said. "Ellie, you can stay with me in exchange for cooking meals and cleaning. You know I am terrible at both, and you would be doing me a favour by agreeing."

"Would sleeping with you also be part of the agreement?" she asked.

"No, of course not," he said quickly. The flash of disappointment in her eyes was so brief he must have imagined it. "I promise you that all I'll require of you are meals and cleaning."

She hesitated, glancing at the door before staring at him again. "I - if you are certain I would be helpful and not a burden."

"I am," he said. "I need your help."

She hesitated a moment longer before nodding. "Then I accept. Thank you."

He reached to take the clothes from her arms, wincing when his swollen knuckles brushed against them. She frowned before taking his hand.

"Oh, Caleb. Your hand – is it broken?"

He shook his head. "Only swollen and sprained, I think. Don't worry about it."

He took her clothes and bag from her and set them on the sofa. "I need to do morning chores. I'll return shortly, and we'll have breakfast, all right?"

She nodded and he smiled at her as he pulled on his jacket and left.

* * *

WHEN HE RETURNED OVER AN HOUR LATER – IT WAS impossible to use his swollen hand to milk Ruby or feed the horses and the oxen, and he'd done everything with just his left – a foul smell permeated the house. He wrinkled his nose, and Scout made a snuffling, sneezing noise before sniffing gingerly in the air.

"Don't worry," Ellie said. "That isn't your breakfast."

"What is it?" he asked as he sat at the table.

"A poultice for your hand," she said absently as she scooped the round ball of cloth from the boiling water. She waited for it to cool a little before squeezing some of the liquid out. "It has different spices to help draw out the pain and the swelling."

She set his plate of food in front of him before taking his hand and placing it on the table. "Keep this on for at least fifteen minutes," she said before plopping the hot poultice on his hand.

He hissed at the pain, and she patted his shoulder gingerly. "Sorry, I know it hurts."

She sat across from him and picked at her food as he ate clumsily with his left hand. "Ellie," he said, "you need to eat."

She smiled wanly at him. "I am eating."

"Not enough," he said.

She took a few bites of meat and eggs to satisfy him

before pushing away her plate. When he was finished, she washed and dried the dishes as Caleb stared silently at the poultice on his hand.

"Does it feel better?" she asked.

"Surprisingly, yes. Where did you learn to do this?"

She shrugged. "My mother knew many ways to heal using spices and plants. My father used to tease her, said that she should have been the - "

She stopped and, her face twisting, plucked the poultice from his hand and deposited it back into the pot of water. "That's good for now. Later this afternoon, you should use it again."

Her voice was steady enough, but he stood and touched her back gingerly. She jerked away, and hurt flashed through him. "Tell me what's wrong."

"My father is – is not the person I thought he was, and I am having a hard time with it," she said. "If Mama were alive, she would never have let him kick me out. I thought he loved me. He wasn't very affectionate, but Mama always said it wasn't his nature to show affection, so I truly believed he loved me. What a foolish little girl I was. He said terrible things to me – said that my virginity was the only - "

She stopped abruptly and turned to face him. "I'm sorry. You are the last person I should be speaking to about my petty troubles with my father. Forgive me."

"I don't mind," he said honestly.

She laughed bitterly. "Nothing my father has done to me will ever compare to what he did to you. It is incredibly selfish to expect you to listen to me whine. I promise it won't happen again."

"You need to talk about it," he said.

"I don't," she replied briefly. "So my father does not love me – there are worse things to endure."

"Ellie - "

She slipped around him and walked to the bookshelf. "May I borrow a book?"

He nodded, and she picked out a book before walking to the guest bedroom. "I think I will read for a while and then have a short nap. I'm feeling a little tired."

* * *

SHE DIDN'T LEAVE HER BEDROOM UNTIL HE LEFT TO DO THE evening chores. He frowned when she tugged on her boots and grabbed her jacket.

"What are you doing, Ellie?"

"I'm going to help you," she said.

He shook his head. "Stay inside where it's warm."

"No," she said stubbornly. "It will take you twice as long with your injured hand. I can be useful to you."

"Ellie, it's not easy to - "

"I am not the fragile flower you believe me to be," Ellie said. "Let me help, please? I want to help."

Her tiny, pleased smile when he nodded in defeat warmed his entire body. She followed him on the path he had made from the house to the barn and looked around curiously when they entered the building.

"This is nice," she said thoughtfully. "You don't have as many animals as I thought."

He shrugged. "I don't need that many with it just being me. Ruby provides the milk, the hens provide the eggs, and the oxen pull the plow for the wheat field and the garden."

"Where do you get your meat?" she asked.

"I hunt most of it. I also buy a pig in the spring and slaughter it in the fall."

"What should I do first?"

"You can feed the hens and Ruby while I feed the horses and the oxen," he said.

Half an hour later, all that was left to do was milk Ruby. He was impressed by Ellie's willingness to help. She had even cleaned out the manure in Ruby's stall before spreading fresh hay. It was obviously difficult for her. Her face was bright red, and sweat was pouring down her face, but she refused to allow him to take over when he finished cleaning the other stalls. The pleased look on her face when she was done made him grin.

He sat on the stool next to Ruby, rested his head against her warm side and tried milking her with his right hand. The poultice had reduced quite a bit of the swelling, and even the pain had diminished a little, but the moment he tried to squeeze Ruby's teat, pain flared through his knuckles. He cursed under his breath before milking her with just his left.

Like this morning, Ruby turned her head to stare at him. The cow was obviously wondering why he behaved oddly with her milking.

"If you show me how to do that, I'll milk her," Ellie said.

"It's harder than it looks," he warned.

She shrugged. "I'm tougher than I look, remember?"

He hesitated before standing and moving back so Ellie could take his place on the stool. She placed her hands on Ruby's teats, and the cow made a startled 'moo.' Ellie jerked and removed her hands before giving the cow an apologetic look.

"Sorry, cow. My hands are cold."

She rubbed her hands together as Caleb smothered his laughter. "Ruby."

"I'm sorry?"

"Her name is Ruby."

"Oh, right. Well, Ruby," she said before gently stroking the cow's side, "remember this is my first time, so don't judge."

Caleb laughed, and she smiled faintly at him. "What's the best technique?"

"Start from the top of her teat and squeeze down with firm pressure."

"Right. Sounds easy," she said.

Two minutes later, she stopped squeezing Ruby's teats and gave him a look of frustration. "What am I doing wrong?"

"Here," he squatted behind her and put both arms around her, placing his left hand on one teat before using his injured hand to guide Ellie's hand to another.

"Watch," he said and firmly squeezed until milk squirted into the bucket beneath Ruby's udder. He repeated it, and Ellie tried with her right. After a few fumbled attempts, she found the technique, and they milked Ruby in tandem until her udder was empty.

He was still crouched behind her, with his chest brushing against her back, when she turned her head to smile delightedly at him. "I did it!"

"You did," he said. "Very good job."

"Thanks. It makes my hand hurt." She rubbed at her right hand, and he studied the way her dark hair gleamed in the light from the lantern. He could feel the heat from her body and smell the faint scent of her soap. God, he wanted her so badly.

"Yes," he said a little hoarsely, "it takes some time to get used to."

"Caleb? Are you all right?" she asked.

Her eyes widened as she registered how close their faces were to each other, and her gaze dropped to his mouth. His cock hardened at the obvious need in her eyes. When she licked her lips and parted them invitingly, he leaned forward and trapped her between his body and Ruby's warm side.

"Please kiss me, Caleb."

Her moaned plea set his blood on fire. He wanted to kiss her. Hell, he needed to kiss her. He would go crazy if he didn't. He dipped his head, but before he could claim her mouth, she was squirming free and backing away.

"I – I'm so sorry," she gasped. "That was inappropriate, and I won't do it again."

"Ellie, wait," he said, but she had already backed out of the stall and headed to the barn door.

"If you don't need any more help, I'll return to the house and start dinner." Her voice was high-pitched and wavering with unshed tears, and he cursed under his breath before nodding.

"That's fine. I'll see you in a few minutes."

CHAPTER 8

Caleb hesitated at the door to the house. Scout whined and pawed at the door, and he petted him absent-mindedly. It had been a week since he brought Ellie back to his home. An entire week of her doing her best to avoid him in the small house. A week of her sitting silently by the fire for most of the day and a week of him trying desperately to ignore his growing urge to touch her, to kiss her and…

Fuck her. You want to fuck her until she's screaming your name. Until she's so weak from coming that she can't get out of your bed.

Yes, he did. He was a horrible person. Ellie diligently avoided being close to him after that moment in the barn last week. She didn't touch him at all, and he never saw desire on her face when she looked at him.

He couldn't blame her. She was still reeling from her father's betrayal and having a difficult time coping with it, but she refused to talk to him about it. He was thankful that she didn't know about her father trying to sell her virginity to Frederick. She was already hurting enough, and he would do everything in his power to make sure she never discovered that particularly horrible piece of information.

"Which is why I'm a son of a bitch," he muttered to Scout. "She's upset and traumatized, and all I can think about is getting between her legs. It's getting harder and harder not to touch her or kiss her. Maybe we should start living in the barn? What do you say, boy?"

The dog cocked his head before pawing at the door again, and Caleb sighed. "Thanks for your support."

He walked into the house. It was warm and smelled delicious, and Ellie stood at the counter. Without turning around, she said, "Breakfast is almost ready. You should wash up."

"Sure," he grunted. He removed his jacket and boots and moved to the basin and jug sitting on a stand next to the woodstove. The water in the jug was warm, and he shook his head. Ellie really did think of everything when it came to taking care of him. She would make an excellent wife.

She really would, my darling, Missy agreed in his head.

Not for me, he argued. *Just in general.*

Oh, of course, Missy said.

He rolled his eyes at his dead wife's voice before pouring water into the basin. The front of his shirt was filthy. One of the hens was limping this morning, and he had gotten dirt and hay, and he suspected chicken shit, all over the front of his shirt when he had cornered her and picked her up to examine her foot.

He quickly unbuttoned his shirt and draped it on the chair before washing his face, chest, arms and hands. Water dripping down his broad chest, he reached for the towel and dried his face. He started drying his upper body and turned when Ellie called his name.

"Do you want two eggs or three this morning?" She added

the eggs he had collected this morning to the basket on the counter.

"Three, please."

* * *

ELLIE GLANCED AT CALEB AND COMPLETELY FORGOT WHAT they were talking about. He stood half-naked in front of her. Water dripped down his broad chest, and her pulse pounded in her ears as she watched a drop slide past one flat nipple.

She was doing a remarkable job the last week of denying her need for him, but seeing him now, seeing his naked skin and that hard body that felt so good against her soft one, made her legs tremble. She knew Caleb wanted her. More than once, she had caught him looking at her with that familiar hunger in his eyes, but she had purposely ignored it.

She wasn't entirely sure why Caleb still lusted after her, but she imagined it was probably because she was a warm female who had already thrown herself at him. They had no future together. He didn't want to marry her, and if she gave in and had sex with him, sooner or later she would get pregnant. Then what would happen? She was already a social pariah. She could only imagine how much worse it would be as an unwed mother.

Still, she reasoned, Caleb had been very kind to her and it would be nice of her to help alleviate some of his obvious need for her. She didn't have to sleep with him. There were other ways to help ease his desire.

But that won't do anything for us! Her inner voice pouted. *What about our needs?*

We don't deserve it. After what my father did to him, I should be doing everything I can to make it up to him. This is what he wants most. I know it is.

You've gone mad, Ellie. What you're saying makes no sense.

You're not responsible for your father's choices. You're doing this because you want him so badly that you're willing to give up your pleasure to see his. Admit it.

She ignored her inner voice's logical reply and gazed up at Caleb. God, she did want him badly. Her entire pelvis was throbbing, and her core was soaking wet just looking at him.

"Ellie? What's wrong?" He was frowning at her, and she could only imagine the look on her face.

"Nothing," she said before walking toward him. "Nothing's wrong, Caleb."

She smoothed her hand down his chest before pressing her mouth against his warm skin and licking at the drops of water.

* * *

CALEB MOANED LOUDLY AS ELLIE, A STRANGE COMBINATION OF anger and desire on her face, pressed her mouth to his chest and licked away the droplets of water. He dropped his hands to her waist, and she pushed him backward until he was pressed against the wall. Her hands curled around his wrists, and she tugged his arms above his head.

"Don't move," she whispered.

"I want to touch you," he muttered.

"No." She shook her head. "Keep your arms above your head."

She traced one flat nipple with her nail before pinching it. His back arched, and he made a low hiss of pleasure. His cock was huge and throbbing in his pants. Just the pressure of his pants was almost enough to make him come.

He started to drop his arms, he was desperate to touch Ellie's breasts, and she pinched his nipple again. "Keep them above your head," she warned in a low voice.

Fresh desire filled him. There was something strangely

erotic about Ellie taking control. He pressed his arms against the wall as she trailed her fingers down his chest and stroked his abdomen. He arched again into her touch, and a small smile crossed her face.

"You want me, don't you, Caleb?"

"Yes," he said hoarsely, "very much."

"Why?"

He hesitated, and she shook her head. "Never mind. It doesn't matter."

"Ellie - "

"Shh," she demanded, and he shut his mouth with a snap when she stroked the waistband of his pants. His cock twitched, and he held his breath as she unbuttoned his pants. She tugged them open and made a soft noise of appreciation when she saw his cock. He was so erect it was almost painful, and the tip was weeping copious amounts of precum. He moaned loudly when her soft hand traced his stomach just above the head of his cock.

"Please, Ellie," he rasped. "Touch me."

He cried out when her hand wrapped around his hard shaft and squeezed firmly. She stroked him once, twice, and then shamefully, his hips were arching, and he was coming all over her hand. She continued to stroke him, milking his cock until the last of his seed had surged out, and he fell back against the wall. He was panting harshly, and he watched silently as she grabbed the towel and quickly cleaned his cock before tucking him back into his pants.

When she turned away and washed her hands before picking up the eggs, he finally moved away from the wall.

"What are you doing?" he asked.

"Making breakfast," she said.

"Forget breakfast. You're coming to the bedroom with me." He reached for her, and she backed away, holding the basket of eggs like a shield.

"I can't."

"Like hell, you can't," he said. "Ellie, my bedroom – now."

She shook her head again. "No."

He glared at her. "If you think I'll let you do something like that without returning the favour, you're wrong. I know you want me. Let me - "

"I can't," she said abruptly. "Leave me be, Caleb. Please."

"No," he said. "Tell me why you're being so," he searched helplessly for the word, "stubborn."

"I don't deserve it!" she snapped at him.

He stared at her. "What the hell does that mean?"

Before she could reply, there was a knock on the door.

Ellie's face paled, and she gave him a frightened look. "W-who is that?"

She thought it was her father or Frederick, perhaps. The fear in her face renewed his rage toward the both of them. He stalked angrily to the door. If it were either of them, he would make them regret stepping one foot on his farm. He yanked open the door, ready for battle, and stared in surprise at the woman standing before him.

She was short and chubby with carefully styled blonde hair and dark brown eyes. She made a soft squeak of fear at the look on his face and took a step back.

"Who are you?" he asked rudely.

"I'm looking for Ellie Walters," she said nervously. "My – my name is Louise Handon."

"Louise?" Ellie pushed past him and threw her arms around the woman. "What are you doing here?"

"I came to visit you," Louise said as she hugged Ellie tightly. "I've been so worried about you."

"You came by yourself?" Ellie scanned the empty yard. "Louise, that's dangerous."

"Of course not, silly," Louise said. "My brother is visiting the Randall's - you know he's courting their oldest daughter

Rebecca - and escorted me here. Mr. Thornwell's farm is not far from theirs."

"How did you convince your mother to allow you to come here?" Ellie asked.

Louise flushed. "Well, she doesn't exactly know. She thinks I'm visiting the Randall's as well."

"Oh, honey," Ellie said. "You shouldn't have done that. What if your mother finds out?"

"She won't," Louise said. "My brother swore he wouldn't say anything. Besides, I don't care even if she does. What she said and did to you was awful, and I've been terribly upset with her for the last week. She shouldn't have said those nasty things to you, Ellie."

Ellie hugged her again, and Louise picked up the bag at her feet. "My brother has ridden on to the Randall farm. He's spending the night and will return to escort me home in the morning. If it's too much of a burden for me to spend the night, I can walk to the Randall's later this afternoon."

She glanced timidly at Caleb, and he immediately shook his head. "Of course not. You're more than welcome to spend the night here."

"Thank you, Mr. Thornwell," she said. Her eyes skittered over his naked chest, and he cleared his throat before stepping back.

"My pleasure. Please, come inside. It's too cold to linger outside."

Holding Louise's hand tightly, Ellie led her into the house. "I was about to make breakfast. Are you hungry?"

Louise shook her head as Ellie took her jacket and hung it on the hook. "No, my brother and I ate before we left. But I could help you cook if you'd like?"

"I would like that," Ellie said happily. "Oh, Louise, I've missed you."

"I've missed you too," Louise said. She followed Ellie into the kitchen as Caleb grabbed a fresh shirt from the bedroom.

He had just sat on the sofa when there was a second knock at the door. Ellie tensed again, and he gave her a reassuring look before walking to the door. He swung it open, and his tension eased when he saw Joseph.

"Hello, Joseph."

"Hello, Caleb. How are you?"

"Good," Caleb replied. "Come in out of the cold."

"Thanks." Joseph stepped inside and unbuttoned his jacket. "I thought I would drop by for a visit. It's been a while, and I figured you're probably as bored as I am, what with this blasted, never-ending weather."

He paused as he caught sight of Ellie and Louise standing in the kitchen, and a wide grin crossed his face. "Perhaps you're not as bored as I thought."

Before Caleb could reply, Joseph crossed the room and stretched his hand to Louise. "Joseph Billings, ma'am."

"Louise Handon. It's nice to meet you, Mr. Billings," she said. Her face was a soft pink, and Joseph's smile widened as he gently clasped her hand and shook it.

"Please, call me Joseph."

He continued to hold her hand as his eyes lingered on her full breasts and then her hips. Her blush deepening, Louise tugged it free, and Joseph turned to Ellie.

"Ellie Walters," she said.

His grin faltered a little, and he glanced at Caleb before shaking Ellie's hand briefly. "You're the doctor's daughter."

"Yes," she said quietly.

There was an awkward silence, and Caleb hurried forward. "We were about to have breakfast, Joseph. Will you join us?"

Joseph nodded. "Yes. I had breakfast earlier, but," he smiled at Louise, and her gaze dropped to his midsection when he patted his lean abdomen, "a bachelor like myself never turns down a meal cooked by such lovely ladies."

Caleb grinned at Joseph and beckoned for him to follow him to the sofa. As they sat down, Joseph glanced again at Louise before saying in a low voice, "I thought you were returning Ms. Walters to her father."

"He kicked her out," Caleb said quietly.

"So, you brought her back here?" Joseph asked.

"She had no place else to go."

"Is that the only reason?"

Caleb didn't reply, and Joseph glanced at Ellie and Louise again. "That doesn't explain why Miss Handon is here as well."

"She's Ellie's best friend, and she stopped in to visit."

Joseph grinned at him. "I'm surprised her father allowed her to visit unaccompanied."

Caleb cleared his throat. "She may have misinformed him about who she was visiting."

Joseph's grin widened. "Beautiful and devious. My favourite combination."

"Behave, Joseph," Caleb warned.

"Says the man who has an unmarried woman living in his home," Joseph said teasingly.

"I'm doing Ellie a favour. She's cooking and cleaning in exchange for a place to live," Caleb replied.

"That's kind of you," Joseph said. "How long will this arrangement go on for?"

"I don't know," Caleb admitted. "She has no money and no other family here."

He studied Ellie for a moment. She was speaking quietly to Louise. Louise shook her head, and a soft smile crossed Ellie's face. Relief flowed through him. Ellie looked happy for the first time since he'd brought her back to his home.

"How long have you been in love with her?"

He blinked in surprise and gave Joseph a guarded look. "I'm not in love with her."

"Aren't you?"

"No," Caleb said. He cleared his throat again before changing the subject. "How is your mother doing?"

* * *

ELLIE HID HER SMILE AS LOUISE, BLUSHING FURIOUSLY, TURNED and grabbed the basket of eggs on the counter. She stood beside her and lightly elbowed her as Caleb and Joseph sat on the sofa.

"Louise," she whispered.

"What?" Louise whispered back.

"Joseph is very handsome."

"He's somewhat pleasing to the eye," she said before glancing at the back of Joseph's dark head.

"He likes you," Ellie said.

"Hush, Ellie. He doesn't," Louise said with a shake of her head. "Besides, his behaviour was very improper. Did you see the way he ogled me?"

Ellie smiled at her. "He did seem rather forward in expressing his interest in you."

"Hush," Louise said. "I have no interest in Mr. Billings."

"Why not?" Ellie asked.

"Could you imagine what mother would say if I fell in love with a farmer?" Louise said. "She'd lock me away in the root cellar or kick me out of -"

She stopped abruptly and gave Ellie a look of horror. "Forgive me, Ellie. I did not mean to speak so carelessly."

"It's fine," Ellie said.

"Your father is a fool," Louise said. She glanced at Joseph and Caleb before lowering her voice. "Mr. Barns is still recovering from Mr. Thornwell's vicious attack. Your father told my father that he did not believe Mr. Barns' nose would heal properly, and his eyes are so swollen that he still cannot see."

"Good," Ellie said with uncharacteristic malice. "He deserved it."

"He did," Louise said. "My father says that the sheriff visited Mr. Barns, but he refused to press charges against Mr. Thornwell. That's odd, isn't it?"

"I suppose," Ellie said. She wondered if Louise could see the relief on her face. She'd worried for over a week now that Caleb would be arrested for attacking Frederick. To know that he wouldn't set her mind at ease.

"I wonder why he didn't," Louise said.

"Perhaps because he knew I would speak to the sheriff about what he tried to do to me," Ellie said. "If the sheriff knew that Frederick attacked me, it would change his view of him."

"If he believed you," Louise pointed out morosely.

"It doesn't matter," Ellie said. "He isn't pressing charges against Caleb, so we don't have to worry."

"True," Louise said. "Are you still sleeping with him?"

"Hush," Ellie said with a quick look at Caleb. "We will speak of it later, all right?"

"All right," Louise said.

* * *

"This has been a truly enjoyable day," Joseph said as he stood from the sofa, "but it's growing late, and I have chores to do."

He buttoned his coat and held out his hand to Ellie. "Miss Ellie, it was a pleasure. Thank you for such a delicious breakfast."

"As well as lunch and dinner," Caleb said with a small grin.

Ellie smiled at Joseph. "You're welcome. It was lovely to meet you."

"You as well," Joseph said. He turned to Louise and took her hand, pressing his mouth against her knuckles. Ellie watched as a soft flush crept up her neck, but she made no move to pull her hand free of Joseph's.

"Miss Louise," Joseph said in a tone entirely different from the one he used with Ellie. "It was a real pleasure to meet you."

"Mr. Billings," she said with a nod.

He was still holding her hand, and Ellie quickly looked at Caleb. He was watching Louise and Joseph with a small grin on his face. As Joseph kissed Louise's hand again, Caleb glanced at Ellie and winked. She bit her bottom lip to keep her laughter from spilling out as Louise stared intently at Joseph.

"I don't go to town often," Joseph said, "but I wondered if I might call on you the next time I am."

Ellie could barely stop her mouth from dropping open when Louise nodded. "I would like that very much, Mr. Billings."

A broad smile crossed Joseph's face. "I'll see you soon then, Miss Louise."

He held her hand for a moment longer before finally dropping it and heading toward the door. He shook Caleb's hand and patted Scout on the flank before leaving.

"Be careful, Joseph," Caleb called before closing the door against the cold wind.

He smiled at Ellie and Louise. "It's still early. How about a game of cards?"

* * *

"GOODNESS, IT'S SO COLD," LOUISE SAID AS SHE CLIMBED INTO the bed next to Ellie and buried her face between Ellie's shoulder blades. "How do you sleep when it's this cold? I'm surprised you haven't frozen to death."

Shivering wildly, Ellie pulled the covers up to her chin. "Tonight is particularly cold, I think. It's not usually this bad. If it is, I sleep by the fire."

"You're not sleeping with Caleb, then?" Louise said bluntly.

Ellie shook her head. "No, of course not."

"Why not?" Louise asked. "He likes you. I can see it in the way he looks at you."

"He wants to sleep with me," Ellie said, "but nothing beyond that."

"I don't believe that's true," Louise said before squishing closer to Ellie.

"It is," Ellie insisted. "Honestly, I don't even know why he wants me in that manner. What my father did to him…"

She trailed off, and Louise squeezed her gently. "Have you spoken to your father at all?"

"No. Caleb returned me to the house so I could get some of my things, but I didn't speak to him. He's made no effort to contact me."

"I'm sorry," Louise said.

"As am I," Ellie said. "But what's done is done, and I have wallowed in self-pity long enough. I need to decide what to do. It was kind of Caleb to offer me shelter in exchange for cooking and cleaning but I need to make money if I am to return to the East."

"You're leaving?" Louise sat up and gave Ellie a shocked look.

"I am," Ellie said. "My mother's sister lives in the East and would take me in. Now that my father has disowned me, there is nothing here for me."

Louise studied her for a moment. "There is Caleb."

"I told you, he feels nothing but lust for me. He told me himself that he would never take me as a wife. He says I'm too fragile to be a farmer's wife. Besides, he only took my virginity as revenge for what my father did to him."

"Then why does he look at you like he cares for you?" Louise asked.

"You're seeing something that isn't there because you're a romantic," Ellie said. "Lie down, Louise. You're letting the cold air under the quilt."

Louise curled up behind her again. "All right. So, we need to figure out how you can make money. Could you convince Caleb to pay you for your services?"

Ellie shook her head. "No. Caleb doesn't have much money, and besides, after all he has done for me, I can't ask him for wages."

"All he has done for you? You mean how he took your virginity and caused your father to kick you out? Ellie, you're in this predicament because of Caleb. I believe he cares for you, but do not forget why you are homeless. You have every right to ask him for a wage for your services."

"It isn't his fault," Ellie said harshly. "I told you before that I seduced him. I wanted him to take my virginity so that Frederick would no longer be interested in courting me. I mistakenly believed my father loved me and would care for me no matter what."

"I'm sorry," Louise said quietly.

"It doesn't matter," Ellie said. "Even if I had suspected what my father's reaction would be, I would still have gone ahead with my plan. Frederick is an evil man, and I would rather be where I am now than be married to him."

She sighed and burrowed deeper under the covers. "But I must accept the fact that sooner or later, Caleb will look for a wife, and I'll be homeless again."

"What will you do?" Louise asked.

"I'm going to return to the saloon and ask Millie for employment again," Ellie said.

"No!" Louise said. "Ellie, you can't do that."

"I have no choice. If we lived in a city or even a larger town, I might find employment as a governess or maybe a washerwoman or seamstress. But my options are limited here. Working in the saloon is the only way to make enough money to leave this place."

"Oh, Ellie," Louise whispered. "I'm so sorry."

"It's fine," Ellie said with a confidence she didn't feel. "I made my choice, and now I must live with the consequences."

"It isn't fair," Louise said. "You don't deserve this."

"The sins of the father are visited upon the children," Ellie said under her breath.

"What did you say?" Louise asked.

"Nothing," Ellie said. "Enough about my troubles. Let's talk about Joseph and how he'll be calling on you."

Louise giggled softly. "My mother will have a fit, but I couldn't resist. He's so charming and handsome, don't you think?"

"Yes," Ellie said. Personally, she thought Joseph didn't hold a candle to Caleb's rugged good looks, but Louise was right in that he was very charming.

"Could you be happy living on a farm?" she asked.

"I think so, with the right husband," Louise said with another giggle. "Besides, it's too soon even to talk that way. Joseph only asked for permission to call on me. He didn't ask for my hand in marriage."

"He seems rather smitten with you," Ellie said.

"I know," Louise said. She paused before saying quietly, "I don't know why. I'm so much chubbier than other women. Mother says I just need to eat less, but I hardly eat anything now."

"You're perfect the way you are. Joseph likes you because you're sweet and gorgeous and lovely," Ellie said.

"Thank you, Ellie," Louise said. She hugged her tightly before yawning and burying her face in Ellie's back again. "I'm so glad I got to see you. I've missed you."

"I've missed you too," Ellie said.

She stared silently into the darkness as Louise's breathing deepened and her arm relaxed around her waist. She wondered if Caleb was lying awake in his bed, wondered if he was thinking about her and what she had done to him earlier. Was he touching himself? Was he wishing she was in his bed with him?

She sighed and buried her head under the covers. There was no point in thinking that way. She couldn't sleep with Caleb again, and believing she could was madness. After Louise left, she would speak to him about returning to the saloon. He would be angry and upset about it, but she was a grown woman who could make her own choices.

CHAPTER 9

"Caleb? What's wrong?" Ellie gave him a startled look when he ran into the house and slammed the door behind him.

He grabbed the rope coiled neatly on the floor next to the door. "There's another blizzard coming in. It looks like a bad one."

He ran back outside, and Ellie hurried to the window. Caleb had tied one end of the rope to the house and was hurrying to the barn, uncoiling the rope behind him as he went. She peered to the left, her eyes widening at the dark clouds gathering in the sky. Already hard flakes of snow were pinging against the glass. She watched Caleb tie a second rope from the house to the outhouse. He was returning to the house when the blizzard hit. The wind rattled the glass in the panes, and the light blotted out instantly as the snow fell fast and furiously.

She lit the candles on the kitchen table and stirred the stew on the woodstove. Caleb opened the door, and Scout barked loudly before shaking the snow from his fur and running to the fire. The wind blew out two of the candles and she relit them as Caleb removed his boots.

"That hit fast," he said.

"Do you think Louise and her brother are all right?" Ellie said worriedly.

Caleb nodded. "Yes. They left early this morning and would have been in town at least two hours ago."

"Thank goodness," Ellie said.

"That smells good," Caleb said.

She smiled at him. "It's not quite ready yet. It'll be finished by the time you return from the chores."

"I did the chores early," Caleb said as he washed his hands. "As soon as I saw the blizzard coming, I started them."

"That was a smart idea," Ellie said.

"Thanks."

There was an awkward silence, and Ellie quickly stirred the stew again. She was feeling an odd combination of relief and nervousness. She had planned to speak to Caleb this evening about returning to the saloon, but there was no point with the blizzard. She couldn't go anywhere until it ended.

No, you can't, her inner voice whispered. *So why don't you ask Caleb if he'd like you to suck on his cock. It's a pleasant enough way to pass the time.*

Her face flushed a brilliant red, and she clenched her hand around the wooden spoon. Her thoughts about Caleb were becoming progressively dirtier, and she was both ashamed and aroused by them.

"What's wrong?"

She stepped back when Caleb's low voice spoke next to her.

"N-nothing," she said.

"You're about to break that spoon," he pointed out. He

took it from her and searched her face as she blushed even more.

"Your face is very red."

"Standing for too long over the stove," she lied. She tried to take the spoon from him and stiffened when his fingers wrapped around her wrist instead. He rubbed his thumb over her rapid pulse, and she stifled the moan that wanted to escape.

"Ellie," he said, "we should talk about what happened yesterday morning."

She shook her head, her need for Caleb flashing like wildfire through her veins, and pulled free of his grip. "No, I'd rather not."

"We need to."

"We don't," she insisted. "It was a mistake and an error in judgment on my part. I promise it won't happen again."

"What if I want it to happen again?" he asked. "What if I want to take you to my bed, strip off your clothes, and bury my cock in your warm, tight pussy?"

Her pussy throbbed in pleasure at his words, and she clamped her thighs together before shaking her head again. "I don't want that."

"You do," he said steadily.

She sighed and backed away again. "Fine, I do. But we can't."

"Yes, we can," Caleb said. "I want to make you feel good. Let me."

"No," she said. "Please, can we speak of other things?"

Her entire body trembled as she waited for his reply. She would say yes if he asked her again to join him in his bed. She didn't have the strength to keep resisting him.

He sighed loudly. "Yes. I'm sorry, Ellie. I won't ask you to join me in my bed again."

She wondered if he could see the disappointment that

flashed across her face. If he did, he made no mention of it. Instead, he sat at the table and stared at his callused hands.

"W-would you like some tea?" she asked.

He nodded. "That would be nice. Thank you."

* * *

CALEB SAT QUIETLY AT THE KITCHEN TABLE AS THE WIND howled and moaned, and the house shook from the force of it. The candle on the table flickered, and he blew it out before sitting silently in the darkness. Ellie had retired over an hour ago, and he really should have gone to bed, but the thought of climbing into his cold bed alone soured him to the idea. Already, the house was cold, and he glanced at her closed bedroom door. She would not be warm enough, but it wasn't like he could force her to join him in his bed. Even if he promised not to touch her, she wouldn't believe him. Truthfully, she shouldn't. His need for her had reached a fevered pitch, and he didn't trust himself not to take her if she was in his bed.

He sighed and dropped his head into his hands. There was no point in sitting here in the dark and the cold. He might as well go to bed. If he were lucky, Ellie would get so cold she'd come to him.

You're pathetic. You know that, right? Hoping Ellie will decide that sleeping with you is preferable to freezing to death?

There was the tell-tale squeal of the bedroom door opening, and he froze as Ellie, carrying a pillow and a pile of blankets and wearing only her chemise, tiptoed into the living room. She crept toward the fire. His cock stiffened when she bent to arrange the blankets on the floor in front of the fireplace, and he caught sight of her long, pale thighs. She crawled between the blankets before curling onto her side.

She was obviously freezing, and his hands tightened into

fists. It was foolish of him to think Ellie would join him in bed. He sat quietly and stared at the table as he waited for her to fall asleep. He should have announced his presence the moment she opened her bedroom door, but he was mesmerized by the achingly familiar sight of her pale arms and legs and, frankly, too blinded by lust to remember his manners. If he said something now, it would frighten her badly. It was better to wait quietly until she was asleep.

Ellie made a low moan, and he snapped his head toward her. Although it was too dark for him to see anything but the vague shape of her body under the blankets, his cock went from half-hard to fully erect. It knew exactly what that moan signaled and he was helpless to stop from standing and moving toward the fireplace.

He watched as Ellie flipped onto her back. Her eyes were closed, and he swallowed heavily when she pushed the blankets down to her sternum. Her left hand slid into her chemise and cupped her breast as her hips arched. There were too many blankets for him to see what exactly her right hand was doing, and he wished she would push the blankets down further. Watching Ellie touch herself was suddenly a fantasy he never knew he had.

Instead of pushing away the blankets, she pinched her nipple and then gasped his name in a low voice. The sound of his name on her lips shattered his control, and he immediately stripped off his clothes as she moaned his name again.

Ellie belonged to him, and it was time for her to realize it.

* * *

HER PUSSY THROBBING, ELLIE RUBBED ROUGHLY AT HER CLIT. She pictured Caleb's hard hands on her breasts, kneading and caressing as he pinched her nipple. She moaned his name, arching her back as her fingers pinched her hard nipple. She rubbed at her clit before turning to her side again. She pressed her thighs together, trapping her hand between them and teased her clit lightly. She was so wet and ready to find the pleasure she was aching for since that moment in the kitchen yesterday. She closed her eyes and brought forth the memory of Caleb coming all over her hand. God, she wished she could go to him. Wished she could have that thick cock sliding into her. It was the only thing that would relieve the never-ending and maddening ache in her pussy.

There was a blast of cold air as the blankets were shifted back, and then a hard body was lying down behind her. Caleb's rough hand curled around her throat and gently pulled her back against him. She yanked her hand out from between her legs and tried to adjust the front of her chemise, which had dipped dangerously low.

Caleb's free hand caught hers and held it firmly as she whispered, "What are you doing?"

"Why are you out here, Ellie?" he asked.

"I was cold and wanted to be closer to the fire."

"You were cold," he said.

She nodded and tried to pull away, but his hand tightened around her throat and held her completely immobile. Oh God, she loved being trapped against him much more than she should have. Knowing that Caleb was firmly in control brought fresh moisture to her core. She was finding it nearly impossible to keep her fingers from slipping between her thighs again.

He tucked her left arm behind her back. He leaned forward, trapping her arm between her back and his chest before reaching around and pulling down the front of her chemise. He tucked it below her breasts, and she made a token noise of objection that he ignored.

"You do look cold, Ellie," he said as he studied her hard

nipples. She moaned loudly when he cupped her breast with his left hand and pulled on her nipple. He pushed his right hand under her neck and curled his fingers around her throat again. He held her steady as he used his other hand to pinch and pull both of her nipples until they were swollen and a dark red.

She was still trapped against him. She supposed if she really tried, she could wiggle her right arm free from where it lay beneath her, but there was something darkly delicious about being pinned against Caleb's hard body. Pretending to be completely helpless against him and pretending that any moment now, he would turn her onto her back and fuck what was his made her pussy throb heavily. If she kept this up, she would think her way to an orgasm.

"Were you touching yourself?" Caleb asked.

She jerked against him and immediately shook her head no.

His hand left her breast and gripped her chin tightly, turning her head toward him so he could angle his mouth over hers. He kissed her hard, forcing her lips apart so he could explore the warmth of her mouth. She moaned happily and rubbed her ass against his cock. Too soon, the kiss was over, and she licked her swollen lips and stared helplessly at Caleb's mouth as he smiled.

"You shouldn't lie to me, Ellie."

"I wasn't," she lied again.

This time, his hand cupped her breast and tugged sharply on her nipple. She squealed at the combination of pleasure and pain, and he pressed a light kiss against her mouth.

"I was in the kitchen the entire time, sweetheart," he said.

Her face turned bright red, and she struggled to free herself. "I'm so embarrassed," she moaned. "Please, Caleb, please let me go."

"No," he said firmly. "You belong to me, and I will no

longer be denied the warmth of your sweet pussy. Not when I know how much it needs me."

"It doesn't need you," Ellie said.

"Doesn't it?" He gave her a smug grin before freeing her left arm and pushing it between her thighs. "Go on then, make yourself come."

"No, I can't," she whispered.

"Yes, you can. You were about to come before I interrupted you," he said. "Go on, Ellie. Touch yourself."

He pushed the blankets off of them and lifted the hem of her chemise to her waist before sliding his arm between her thighs. She jerked when he lifted her top leg, curling his hand around her smooth thigh and lifting her leg until she could feel the strain in her muscles. Her pussy was exposed to the cool air, and she squirmed against him.

"Caleb, please, I - "

"Touch yourself right now, Ellie," he demanded quietly, and she was helpless to deny his order.

She cupped her pussy, rubbing at her clit as he leaned over her and watched. "That's my good girl," he praised. "Slide two fingers into your pussy. You're going to fuck your fingers for me."

She pushed two fingers deep into her aching core and moved them rapidly in and out. Her heart was pounding, and Caleb was tracing the fluttering pulse beneath his hand with light strokes of his fingers.

It felt so good. Not as good as Caleb's cock, but with his hard body behind hers and with his low voice whispering in her ear, she could come like this. She really shouldn't. She had promised herself she wouldn't, but technically she wasn't fucking Caleb, so she wasn't breaking her own rule.

"Does that feel good, my sweet?" he whispered.

"Yes," she muttered as she fucked herself harder.

"But not as good as my cock."

She jerked to a stop when he slid his cock between her legs and rubbed it against the back of her hand.

"Move your fingers, and I'll give you what you really want," he rasped.

"I can't," she moaned. "I don't deserve it."

"Yes, you do," he said into her ear. "You've been such a good girl, cooking my meals and caring for me. Don't you think you should be rewarded for that?"

She squirmed against him, and he stroked her throat before kissing her jaw. "You're my good girl, Ellie. Say it."

"I'm your good girl," she whispered obediently.

He licked the curve of her ear. "And what does my good girl get?"

"Your cock," she moaned.

"That's right. Move your hand."

Her entire body trembling, she moved her hand and cried out when he immediately pushed his cock into her waiting pussy. Still holding her leg high, he fucked her slowly as she squirmed and pleaded for him to move faster.

"Touch yourself," he ordered.

She rubbed at her clit, and it took only a few seconds before the pleasure washed over her. She cried his name, her body shuddering against his as her pussy clenched around his thick shaft in rhythmic pulses. He groaned and then flipped her onto her stomach. She muttered in displeasure at the loss of his cock, but he was hauling her to her knees and crowding his way between her spread thighs. He shoved his cock deep into her pussy as he pulled her chemise over her head and tossed it aside. He pressed one heavy hand between her shoulder blades, forcing her upper body into the blankets and raising her ass.

He squeezed one smooth ass cheek before curling his hand around her hip and holding her firmly. He fucked her with hard, deep strokes as she moaned and pushed back against him. Her hair was hanging in her face, and he gathered it into a ponytail with one hand and gripped it tightly. Each thrust of his cock brought a delicious tension to her scalp, and she clutched at the blankets as Caleb used his large thighs to spread her soft ones even further.

He dug his fingers into her hip before pounding into her. For long moments, there was only the sound of their bodies slapping together, of their tortured breathing and loud moans. Ellie tensed again, her back arching and her body twitching with harsh spasms of pleasure. Caleb groaned, and his hand tightened in her hair before he shoved his cock so deeply inside of her that she collapsed to the floor with a startled cry. He followed her down, his weight pinning her to the blankets as wetness flooded her insides. She squirmed beneath him, but he kept her pinned where she was, sliding his cock back and forth in her pussy as the last of his orgasm flowed through him. It wasn't until his cock softened that he rolled off her. She took a gasping breath as his arm snaked around her waist, and he pulled her into his embrace.

"Do you feel better, my sweet?" he murmured into her hair as he stroked her back.

"Yes, but I shouldn't have done that. We can't do this again," she replied.

"Keep speaking that way, and I will fuck you again right now," he said grouchily. He stood and tugged her to her feet before carrying her to his bedroom.

She should have resisted, but instead, she rested her cheek on his broad chest and closed her eyes. She would have tonight to be in his arms. She would touch him and find pleasure from his touch, and then tomorrow, she would insist that he not touch her again.

* * *

Ellie flipped the last of the pancakes and waited patiently for them to finish cooking. Caleb would be back soon from the morning chores, and she ignored the throbbing in her pussy. She had vowed this morning to return to her original plan. Just because Caleb fucking her three times in the night had only increased her need for him rather than sating it was no reason to abandon her plan. She needed to be stronger and have more willpower.

The door opened in a flurry of wind and snow, and Caleb and Scout swept into the house. He removed his jacket and boots before crossing the room to wash up in the basin by the stove.

"Blizzard is getting worse," he said.

"It sounded worse," she said.

She placed the stack of pancakes on the table beside the maple syrup and gave him a brief smile. "Eat up while they're still warm."

"They smell good," he said cheerfully before sitting down. He frowned when she didn't join him. "Are you not eating?"

"I'm not that hungry this morning," she said. It was true. Her lust for Caleb – and God, how much worse was it now that he was sitting less than two feet from her – had driven away her appetite.

He studied her carefully, and she brushed nervously at her skirt and top. She wasn't wearing petticoats or her drawers, just her thin chemise, and she was aware of how visible her rapidly hardening nipples were.

Had she done that on purpose? Had she specifically worn as little clothing as possible to entice Caleb? She tried to tell herself she hadn't, but as Caleb's nostrils flared and he stood up abruptly, her pussy was instantly wet.

"Caleb, we can't - "

He was on her in a heartbeat, his hands yanking her shirt over her head and shoving her skirt to the floor. He pulled off her chemise before she could even think to stop him – and did she really want to anyway – and stared appreciatively at her naked form.

"Much better," he muttered before cupping her breast and squeezing it gently. She stared mutely at him as his other hand reached between her legs.

He grinned at her wetness. "Feels like my good girl needs to be fucked."

"The pancakes are getting cold," she said in a foolish attempt to deny both her own need and his.

He laughed as he quickly unbuttoned his trousers and pulled out his cock through the opening. He carried her to his chair and sat down, forcing her to straddle him. Her back scraped against the edge of the table as he lifted her with one arm around her waist.

"Caleb, what - "

Her voice cut out as his cock sank into her pussy. He pushed her down until he was sheathed entirely in her warmth and her wetness and grinned when she moaned loudly and clung to his shoulders.

"Oh," she whispered. "Oh."

There was something darkly erotic about Caleb being fully dressed while she was completely naked. Her legs dangled and she could only just touch her toes to the floor. When Caleb spread his legs, she lost even that tenuous grasp. She looked down at where they were connected, and fresh moisture coated his cock and dripped onto his pants.

"I love how wet you are for me, sweetheart," he said.

"Caleb, please," she moaned.

"This? Is this what you need?" He cupped the back of her neck and thrust into her. She gasped and clung to his shoulders.

"Oh, oh yes."

She scowled when he stopped immediately. He winked at her before leaning forward and sliding his arms around her.

"What are you doing?" she gasped when she heard the clink of silverware against his plate.

"You told me to eat the pancakes before they got cold," he reminded her.

He leaned back and showed her the fork in his hand. He had stabbed a piece of pancake and dipped it in syrup, and she watched in disbelief as he popped it into his mouth and chewed slowly.

"You make the best pancakes, Ellie. Have I ever told you that?"

"Caleb, please!" she said in frustration before wiggling on his lap. "Please, I need you."

"No moving, sweetheart," he said before cupping the back of her neck and holding her firmly in his lap. "It's breakfast time, remember?"

"I told you I wasn't hungry!" she snapped.

"Yes, but I am." He grinned.

He leaned forward again and brought forth a second piece of pancake. As he lifted it past her shoulder, a drop of syrup landed on the swell of her breast. He ate his second mouthful as they both watched the syrup slide slowly down her breast to catch on her erect nipple.

He made an appreciative sound in the back of his throat before leaning forward and licking and sucking the syrup from her nipple. Ellie cried out with pleasure, her fingers gripping the collar of his shirt as he thrust into her three times.

"No!" She pounded his back in frustration when he stopped and flushed at his warm chuckle.

"Only my good girl gets fucked with my cock, remember?"

"I'm your good girl," she said immediately before rocking her pelvis against him.

His hand tightened around the nape of her neck. "Good girls eat their breakfast. Did you eat your breakfast, sweetheart?"

She pouted at him even though she was enjoying this game - really enjoying it if the way his pants were darkening from the moisture dripping steadily from her pussy was any indication - and he laughed again.

He cut a third piece of pancake, dipped it in the maple syrup and held it in front of her mouth. She ate it quickly and then squealed happily when Caleb rewarded her with more hard thrusting.

He stopped, and she muttered an unladylike curse under her breath. He held out another forkful of pancake. She ate it and waited expectantly, frowning when he offered her another bite of pancake. She ate that one as well, licking the syrup from her lips and then clinging to him when he fucked her roughly.

He spent the next ten minutes alternating between feeding her bites of pancake and fucking her. She was a moaning, shivering mess by the time he set the fork down, gripped her waist and fucked her the way she was begging him to.

She rode him to a screaming, body-shaking orgasm in less than two minutes. He followed shortly after, sliding his arms around her and pressing her tightly against him as he bucked his hips and came deep inside of her. After when they had both stopped trembling, he made her sit naked on his lap while he ate the rest of the pancakes.

"At least let me put on my chemise," she protested.

He shook his head and slipped his hand between her arm and her ribcage to cup her naked breast. He popped a piece of pancake into his mouth before smiling at her. "I prefer you naked."

She flushed as he toyed lazily with her nipple. "I'll freeze to death."

"I'll keep you warm," he said. "I want you to spend the day naked."

"I can't," she said. "What if someone comes to the house?"

He raised his eyebrows at her. "In the middle of a blizzard?"

"Caleb, I - "

"Try it for me," he said as he rolled her erect nipple between his finger and thumb. "Whenever you get cold, let me know, and I'll warm you."

She hesitated before nodding and the look of pure delight on his face brought a smile to hers.

* * *

ELLIE SHIFTED ON THE SOFA BEFORE DIGGING HER HAND INTO the arm of it. A shiver went through her naked body, and she stared blankly at the crackling fire. She had spent the entire day without wearing a stitch of clothing, and after the initial embarrassment, there was something rather freeing about walking around naked. Caleb had remained fully dressed, and it was shamefully arousing to her whenever their bodies came into contact. What was it about being completely naked and Caleb staying dressed that turned her on so much, she mused. She wasn't sure, but knowing that his cock remained hidden from her while he was free to look at and touch her pussy whenever the urge struck him, made her unbelievably wet.

She shivered again as Caleb stroked her pale thigh. Not that she hadn't seen it today. She had – multiple times. She was beginning to understand just how large Caleb's appetite for sex really was, and she was surprised that hers seemed to match it. He also, she was discovering, had certain tastes that were becoming more apparent. More than once, he had pinned her to the sofa or the bed or – her face flamed – the table while he was fucking her.

He seemed to like it when she was trapped beneath him, squirming with need and unable to get free. She'd lost count of how often he made her tell him she belonged to him. His hard hands holding her down, his raspy voice insisting that her body, her pussy, every part of her belonged to him made her so hot, she could hardly think straight. She supposed she should have been ashamed of her willingness to give up control, but she wasn't. She liked it when he whispered those things in her ear, liked it when he took her whenever and however he wanted.

Had his wife enjoyed it as well? Did he tell the other women he'd taken to his bed since his wife's death that they belonged to him? Her body stiffened, and jealousy flooded through her. Stupidly enough, the thought of Caleb being with his wife hadn't once brought a moment of jealousy, but thinking of the other women who had been with him made her stomach ache. He would have had many, his appetite for sex guaranteed it. She thought back to the saloon girls she had met briefly. Which one of them had been with Caleb? Which of them had felt his warm touch, had taken what belonged to her and only her? Anger started colouring her jealousy now, and she closed her eyes. She knew it was wrong of her to keep sleeping with Caleb, but if it meant keeping other women away from him, she would do so. He was hers now.

"You're shivering." Caleb gave her a naughty grin before pulling her thighs apart and rubbing lightly at her pussy. "Do you need to be warmed up again?"

"How many women have you slept with since your wife died?" she asked abruptly.

He blinked at her in surprise before moving his hand away. "You want to talk about this now?"

She nodded, and he sighed before folding his hands into his lap. "Just you."

"What?" Her mouth dropped open, and he blushed a little.

"You don't believe me?" he asked.

"I – but you…"

He frowned at her. "But I what?"

"You seem to like sex so much," she whispered as a hot flush rose in her cheeks.

He laughed. "I do. Very much."

"But you went two years without it," she said.

He stared into the fire. "I love my wife and would rather have nothing but my hand than soil her memory with another woman."

She recoiled in sudden horror, shame and hurt flooding through her. She had known that Caleb had initially slept with her only to gain his revenge against her father, but there was a small part of her that hoped it meant more than that now. To know that every time he slept with her, he believed he was soiling the memory of his dead wife made her want to vomit.

He glanced at her, his eyes widening at the look on her face. "No, Ellie, I didn't mean it like that."

"It's all right," she said shakily. "Really, it's fine. But I think maybe we should stop, uh, sleeping together."

"No!" He pulled her into his lap and rubbed her back as she sat stiffly against him. "I'm sorry, sweetheart, that was a stupid thing to say."

"It wasn't." She tried to keep her voice from wavering. "It's good to be honest with me, and I appreciate it."

He cursed again and forced her head to his chest, running

his fingers through her long dark hair as he rubbed her side and hip with his free hand. "That was before, Ellie, not now. I felt that way before, which is why I hadn't slept with anyone else. I don't feel that way now. Being with you is amazing, and I have no regrets. I promise."

She sighed shakily and finally relaxed against him. They sat quietly before she said, "Tell me about Missy."

He hesitated, and she stroked his chest. "Please."

"She was shorter than you with blonde hair and blue eyes. She was, uh, curvier than you are," he said.

"I met her," she said. "I know what she looked like. I want to know what she was like as a person."

"Smart," he said. "She was much smarter than me. She loved to laugh and make other people laugh. She spoke her mind and didn't care what others thought, but she was kind too. She went out of her way to make other people happy. Our fathers were best friends, so we grew up together. I knew when I was a teenager that I would marry her. She was," he paused, "sturdy and tough as nails, and I knew she'd be strong enough to go west. I wanted my own land, and Missy encouraged me even though she knew how dangerous it would be. The first couple of years were bad. There was a drought for both years, and our crops died, but Missy wouldn't let me give up. She told me I'd regret it if I gave up on my dreams. She was right."

Ellie closed her eyes. It was easy enough to hear the love in Caleb's voice, and she felt bitter regret for asking him about her. Why had she done that? Did she need to be reminded that she was too fragile to be a farmer's wife, unlike his beloved Missy? Why torture herself, hoping Caleb would love her the way he loved Missy? She was his bed warmer and nothing else. Sooner or later, he would look for an actual wife, one who was strong enough to live on the prairies, and she would be right back where she started. No money and no place to live.

He might learn to love you.

No, he wouldn't. Just because he enjoyed sex with her didn't mean he would fall in love with her. Not anytime soon, anyway.

So what? Where else do you have to go? Keep doing what you're doing, and be patient.

She snorted to herself. She already had a plan. She would return to the saloon and work for Millie. Sleeping with Caleb and cooking his meals while she hoped that he would fall in love with her, or at the very least become attached enough not to allow her to be homeless, was a foolish idea. What a mess her life had turned out to be. Her father hated her, her reputation was destroyed, she was penniless and homeless, and she was in love with a man who would never love her.

Love?

She chewed at her bottom lip as Caleb shifted her on his lap. She wasn't in love with Caleb. She was very fond of him, even if he had only used her to hurt her father, but she wasn't in love with him. That was a slip of the tongue, nothing more.

Liar.

"Ellie? Are you all right?"

She nodded and blinked back the hot tears. Caleb already thought she was weak, and she needed to stop crying around him. "I am. Thank you for telling me about Missy. She sounds like a wonderful person, and I'm so sorry for what my father - "

"Don't," he said harshly. "You are not to blame for your father's actions."

She didn't reply. It was kind of him to say that, but he

didn't mean it. If he had, he wouldn't have taken her virginity as payback.

He didn't want to, remember? He told you no multiple times. He came right out and said it wouldn't be right for him to have sex with you. You convinced him to fuck you. He wouldn't have touched you if you hadn't acted like such a whore. Don't ever forget that, Ellie.

Her head suddenly throbbing, and feeling tired and depressed, she tried to slide from Caleb's lap. His arms tightened around her, and she patted his chest gingerly. "It's getting late. I should probably go to bed."

* * *

WHEN ELLIE TRIED TO SLIDE FROM HIS LAP, CALEB TIGHTENED his arms around her waist. He cupped her face and tilted it toward his, studying it carefully. Her face was very pale, and her eyes shiny with unshed tears, and he cursed to himself. He should never have told her about Missy. It just reminded her of her father and what she had lost, and he hated bringing her pain.

"My bed or yours," he said.

"W-what?"

"Are you planning on going to my bed or yours?"

"Um, my bed?" she said hesitantly as she crossed her arms over her naked breasts.

"Wrong answer, Ellie," he said as he shifted her until she straddled his thighs. He quickly unbuttoned his pants and pulled his cock free before rubbing it against her pussy. She squirmed, and he held her tightly as he rubbed the head of his cock over her clit. When she was wet and moaning softly, he leaned back and cupped her breast. Her hips were rocking back and forth against his cock, and he watched the flush rise in her cheeks.

She stopped abruptly, and he squeezed her waist. "Don't stop."

"Caleb, we've already been together multiple times today," she said.

"Are you sore?" he asked before pressing a kiss against her upper chest.

"No, but I - "

"But what?"

He studied her in the glow from the fire. God, she couldn't hide anything on that expressive face of hers. She believed she needed to deny him sex so that he wouldn't grow tired of her.

Her mouth trembled, and she glanced at the wooden trunk in the corner of the living room. He had tossed the saloon dress on top of it, and neither of them had gone near it since. He could almost read the thoughts flashing across her face. If he lost interest in her, she would have no choice but to return to the saloon. He pulled her roughly against him and pressed the head of his cock against her wet entrance.

"I don't want you to get tired of me," she said.

"I will never grow tired of you, Ellie," he muttered into her ear before sliding his cock deep into her pussy.

She moaned, her back arching. Caleb cupped one full breast before teasing her nipple until it was a hard pebble against his palm. He thrust slowly back and forth, watching the firelight dance across her face as she met each of his thrusts with a slow tilt of her pelvis.

He thumbed her clit, and she made a small breathless shriek of pleasure before gripping his wrist. "Caleb, wait."

He growled at her and she flushed but tugged on his wrist again. "I need to speak with you about something important."

"What?" he asked before rubbing her clit again.

149

She cried out, her fingers digging into his hard flesh. "I – you shouldn't be inside of me when you…"

"When I what?"

Her face flushed. "When you come."

He didn't reply, and she gave him a nervous look. "I'm sorry, but it wouldn't be good if I got pregnant."

Conflicting emotions flickered through him. A fierce protectiveness at the thought that she may already be carrying his child, fear that he would lose her like he lost Missy, and surprisingly, a small thread of anger that she didn't want to have his baby. She belonged to him now, and if she were pregnant, she would never be able to leave him.

He didn't stop to think about why that filled him with such satisfaction. Instead, he sat up and twisted before pushing Ellie onto her back on the narrow sofa. He wasn't gentle, and she made a squeak of surprise as he spread her legs wide and rammed his cock in to the hilt. He pinned her arms above her head and fucked her roughly until she was moaning and bucking her hips up to meet each of his thrusts.

"You are mine to do with as I want," he breathed hotly into her ear. She shuddered beneath him, and her pussy squeezed his cock so tightly he couldn't stop his groan.

She was growing close, he could feel it in the way her pussy fluttered around him, hear it in the hitch of her breath, and he grinned fiercely at her. "Your body is mine, and I will not be denied the pleasure of feeling your pussy squeezing my cock when I come. Do you understand, Ellie?"

"Caleb," she moaned, and he licked one hard nipple before staring at her.

"Do you understand?" He punctuated each word with a hard thrust of his hips, and she nodded frantically.

"Yes! Yes, I understand!"

He reached between them and tugged on her clit. She screamed in pleasure as it threw her over the edge. He groaned again as she came, her body shuddering and her pussy clamping down around him. He thrust and retreated, his hand still pinning her arms above her head until, with a hoarse shout, he came deep inside of her. He kept himself buried deep until the last of his seed was coating her insides before smiling in satisfaction.

CHAPTER 10

Ellie wiped down the counter before flipping the eggs in the pan. Her stomach throbbed, and she winced before pressing her hand against her abdomen. She had woken when Caleb dressed to do the morning chores, and he kissed her lightly before leaving the bedroom. It was two days later, and the blizzard had ended sometime in the night.

She had relaxed in the bed for a few minutes before throwing back the covers. It was then she discovered that her cycle had started. She stared at the sheets in dismay, embarrassment coursing through her, before hurriedly cleaning herself up and adding a soft absorbent cloth to her underclothes. She stripped the bed and placed the sheets in a tub of water to soak. By the time she was finished putting fresh sheets on the bed, her stomach and pelvis were beginning to throb. She'd always had difficult menstrual cycles, and it seemed that this one would be no different.

She cursed loudly. The eggs were burning, and she could feel tears pricking in her eyes as she fished them out of the pan and threw them away.

Don't cry, she told herself fiercely. Don't be such a big baby.

It was sound advice that her mind chose not to heed. The tears streamed down her face as she grabbed more eggs from the basket on the counter. Caleb would be angry with her for ruining breakfast.

No, he won't. You know he won't.

She sniffed miserably and rubbed her aching stomach. She was getting a headache and wanted to return to bed and lie down, but she needed to finish making Caleb's breakfast. He allowed her to stay with him because she cooked and cleaned for him. If she didn't do that, what use would he have for her?

Don't forget the fucking. If you don't think that's a big reason he's letting you stay, you're fooling yourself, Ellie.

She couldn't do that now either, so it was even more important that she finish his breakfast. It didn't matter how badly her back and pelvis were throbbing. She cried again as she cooked the new eggs. God, she hated how emotional her cycle made her. Crying over burnt eggs was stupid.

Is it the eggs you're crying over or the fact that you're not pregnant with Caleb's baby?

Her hand clenched around the egg, and its fragile shell cracked, spilling its insides all over the counter. She cried harder as she cleaned up the fresh mess. Of course she wasn't upset by that, was she? She was happy that she wasn't pregnant. She knew how lucky it was that she wasn't. She'd only had the courage to talk to Caleb once about her worry and look at how that turned out. Oddly, it had made him seem even more determined to be inside of her when he came.

Don't be ridiculous, Ellie. Caleb is not purposely trying to get you pregnant. Why on earth would he do that?

The door opened, and Scout and Caleb entered in a rush of cold air. He hung up his jacket and kicked off his boots before blowing on his cold hands. "Well, the blizzard has ended, but holy hell is it cold out there."

She made a small, noncommittal noise of agreement and tried to ignore her aching lower body and throbbing head. She would finish Caleb's breakfast and then lie down for a while. She still needed to wash the floors, but it would have to wait.

"Ellie?" Caleb's hand touched her back, and she forced herself to smile at him.

"Sorry, breakfast is a little late. I burned the eggs."

He studied her carefully. "Are you ill? You're white as a sheet."

She shook her head. "No, I'm fine."

He touched her forehead. "You're very warm. I think you have a fever."

"I don't," she said quickly. "It's just warm in here."

"No, it isn't," he said. His eyes widened when she grimaced and pressed her hand against her stomach.

"What's wrong?" There was a thin note of panic in his voice, and she tried to smile reassuringly at him.

"Nothing. I," her cheeks flushed, "it's my menstrual cycle."

Disappointment flashed across his face, and she stared miserably at the floor. "I'm sorry."

She hoped he wouldn't ask her for sex anyway. She wasn't comfortable with the idea, and her pelvis and back were aching so badly that she wouldn't enjoy it.

If he asks, you have to say yes.

Caleb said I didn't have to have sex with him to stay here. He said it was just cooking and cleaning.

That was before. Now that you're fucking him every day, do you think he'll be content with letting you live in his home just because you can cook?

"Ellie?"

"I'm sorry?" She realized Caleb had been speaking to her and turned to him. "What did you say?"

"I said you don't have to apologize. But you should lie down for a bit. You're too pale."

"I need to finish cooking breakfast and wash the floors," she said as her back throbbed and her head ached.

"No, you don't," he said. "Lie down. I'll finish up breakfast and bring some to you."

"I'm not very hungry," she said. "Thank you for being so kind."

"Go on," he said gently before kissing her forehead.

He turned to the stove, and feeling miserable and sick, she wandered toward the bedroom. She hesitated, glancing again at Caleb. His back was turned to her, and he carefully stirred the eggs. She pivoted and walked to the guest bedroom. He would not want her in his bed if she couldn't have sex with him.

* * *

CALEB FINISHED HIS BREAKFAST AND THEN WASHED THE FEW dishes. He glanced at his bedroom before pacing back and forth in the living room. He grabbed a book and sat on the sofa but had only read a few pages when he tossed it aside. Scout was staring at him from his place by the fire, and Caleb paced for a few more minutes before pouring a glass of water. He would take Ellie some water, maybe lie down with her and rub her back for a while. Missy had always had long and painful cycles, and it looked like Ellie was the same.

Holding the glass of water, he knocked lightly on the bedroom door before opening it. "Ellie, I have some water for you."

He scowled at the empty bed before leaving the glass of water on the nightstand and stomping to the guest room. He opened it without knocking, and Ellie gasped and sat up. She winced and rubbed her stomach before standing.

"What's wrong? Have I slept too long?" She stared out the window and, hunched over a little, moved toward the doorway. "I'm feeling better. Thank you for letting me rest."

"What are you doing?" He grabbed her arm as she tried to slide by him.

"I'm going to wash the floors."

He shook his head. "Leave them."

"Caleb, I - "

"Why are you in here?"

She gave him a puzzled look. "I was resting."

"Why are you not in my bed?"

"Well, I…"

She trailed off, and he gave her his own puzzled look before suddenly scooping her up and carrying her to his bedroom. He set her on her feet and stripped off his clothes before beginning to strip her down to her drawers. She nervously crossed her arms over her breasts.

"I'm so sorry, but I would prefer if we didn't have sex right now," she said anxiously.

He gaped at her, and she bit her bottom lip. "I'm very sorry. I'll make it up to you when my cycle is over. I promise. It's just that my back and stomach are very sore, and I don't think I would enjoy it."

"You think I'm bringing you in here for sex," he said slowly.

"Well…yes?" she said.

He scowled at her. "Do you think that little of me, Ellie? You think I would force you to have sex with me when you're not feeling well? Do I come across as that unkind?"

He winced when Ellie burst into tears. She sobbed loudly as he gave her a chastised look.

"Sweetheart, don't cry. I'm sorry."

"I – I – I didn't mean to make you angry," she continued to sob. He pulled her into his arms and rubbed her back.

"You didn't," he said.

"I did," she said before crying louder.

Feeling a little bewildered and useless – Ellie rarely cried, and when she did, it wasn't like this – he guided her into his bed before climbing in beside her. He pulled her up against him and tucked the sheet and the quilt around the both of them before rubbing her lower back. She buried her face in his neck and sobbed. After nearly ten minutes, her sobs turned to watery hiccups, and he squeezed her hip lightly.

"Ellie, you know that anytime you don't want to have sex, all you have to do is say so, right?" He could hear the anxiety in his voice. He had taken Ellie many times over the last few days, and she had always seemed willing, but what if she was only doing it because she thought she had no choice? His stomach rolled with nausea at the thought.

Her voice muffled, she said, "Yes, I know."

"Are you sure?" he said. "If you don't want to have sex with me, then - "

"I want to have sex with you," she said. "Just not right now."

He relaxed slightly, and she mumbled. "I'm so sorry. I don't think you're unkind, Caleb. Really, I don't."

"I know," he said. "I shouldn't have said that. I wouldn't expect you to sleep with me during your cycle or when you're not feeling well, sweetheart. I brought you here because my bed is more comfortable, and I thought I would lie down with you."

She made another watery, sobbing gasp, and he rubbed her back again. "It's okay, Ellie."

She leaned back and he studied her flushed cheeks and swollen nose and eyes as she gave him a faint smile. "Father always banished me to my room during my cycle. He said I was an emotional wreck, and he didn't have the patience to deal with it. I guess he was right."

He scowled and pulled her closer. "You're not feeling well. It's normal to be more emotional when you're feeling sick."

He continued to rub her back, and she made a soft moan. "That's really helping."

"Good, I'm glad." He kissed her forehead before tucking her head against his wide neck. "Close your eyes and try to get some rest, sweetheart."

"The floors," she whispered.

"Can wait. Rest, Ellie," he said.

* * *

"ELLIE, THERE'S NO NEED TO WASH THE FLOORS," CALEB SAID with a frown.

"I'm feeling much better," Ellie said. It was five days later, her cycle had finished last night, and she was finally feeling herself again. She scrubbed the floors with a brush as Caleb hurried over.

"You should rest more. I'll finish the floors."

She laughed as he squatted next to her. "Don't be so silly. I promise I wouldn't do this if I didn't feel better."

He studied her anxiously, and she impulsively pressed a kiss against his mouth. "I swear, Caleb."

He grinned at her and cupped her face before kissing her slowly and deeply. When they broke apart, she was flushed, and he kissed the tip of her nose before smiling again at her. "I'm going to the barn for a bit, all right?"

She nodded and tried to ignore her pounding heartbeat. "All right."

He left, and she finished washing the floors before sitting on the sofa and opening the book she had started the previous night. When Caleb returned over an hour later, she was completely absorbed in it and gasped when he sat beside her.

"Hi," she said. She told herself to shift away, but when Caleb put his arm around her, she leaned into him instead.

He rubbed her upper arm lightly. He smelled like hay, and she pressed her face into his shirt and inhaled deeply. He laughed and kissed the top of her head. "I guess I should wash up."

"No, you smell like hay. I like it," Ellie said.

He grinned at her. "A city girl who likes the smell of hay?"

She shrugged. I suppose it's a bit unconventional. Thank you for letting me read your books."

"Of course," he said in surprise. "Are you enjoying that one? It's one of my favourites."

"I'm enjoying it very much," she said. She glanced at the bookshelf before saying, "Have you always loved to read?"

"Yes. My mother was a school teacher, and she taught all of her children a love for reading," Caleb said. "Many of those books come from her collection. She gave them to me as a going away gift when we moved out west."

"So, your parents are still alive?"

"Yes. My mom is still teaching, and my father is a tailor."

"Why did you want to be a farmer?" she asked.

He shrugged. "My grandfather was a farmer, and I spent much of my childhood at his farm. I grew up loving it even though it's a difficult life."

She set her book on the arm of the sofa and smiled at him. "It's good to do what you love."

"It is," he said. He studied her mouth for a moment before clearing his throat. "Are you sure you're feeling better, Ellie?"

"Yes," she said. "Thank you for allowing me to rest so much these last few days. That was very kind of you."

He rubbed her arm again. "Anytime you're not feeling

well, do not trouble yourself with cleaning or cooking. All right?"

She nodded and stared at the floor for a moment. "The hot baths every morning were very helpful. Thank you for doing that. I know it isn't easy to heat and haul the water daily."

"I didn't mind," he said.

Tell him your cycle is over, her inner mind demanded. *Tell him you want to be fucked.*

I will do no such thing!

"Ellie? What's wrong?" Caleb asked.

His fingers were tracing small circles on her upper arm, and the roughness of them sent little tingles of pleasure down her spine.

"Nothing's wrong," she whispered. "I am just, uh…"

She trailed off before suddenly blurting out, "My cycle ended last night, so you will not need to heat the water tomorrow morning."

She stared at the floor as her inner voice cheered happily.

Caleb's hand tightened on her arm, and she forced her gaze to his. She caught her breath at the obvious look of need on his face.

"Caleb, I - "

He leaned forward and kissed her hard on the mouth before wrapping his arm around her waist and pulling her into his lap until she was straddling him.

She moaned and returned his kiss, sucking on his tongue when he pushed it into her mouth. She rubbed her aching core against his erection. He unbuttoned her blouse and pulled it from her body before yanking down the front of her chemise. The delicate fabric ripped at the seams, but she didn't care as Caleb cupped her breasts and kneaded them roughly. He bent his head as she rested her hands on his knees and arched her back, silently begging him to suck her nipples.

She cried out with pleasure when his hot mouth surrounded one throbbing nipple. He licked and sucked at it, rubbing the tip of it against the roof of his mouth before biting it lightly. She moaned and jerked against him, her hands squeezing his legs as he switched to her other nipple.

He kissed her neck and sucked her on her earlobe before grabbing her hands and moving them to the front of his pants. "Unbutton my pants," he growled into her ear.

She unbuttoned them quickly and pulled out his cock, rubbing it roughly as he nipped at her throat before sliding his hands under her skirt and stroking her firm thighs. Her drawers were crotchless, and she cried out again when he cupped her naked pussy and pushed one thick finger into her. She was soaking wet, and he made a growl of approval before pulling her closer.

"Lift your skirt," he demanded.

She hurried to obey him, bunching the material around her waist. He guided his cock to her pussy and rubbed the head of it against her clit as he kneaded and rubbed her breasts with his left hand.

"Do not tease me," she said sharply as she lifted her body.

He grinned at her and pressed his cock against her wet opening. She moaned and drove her body downward, sheathing him entirely in one hard stroke. He groaned loudly when she dropped her skirt and bounced on his lap, driving his cock in and out of her with hard, deep strokes. He pulled her closer and kissed her hard on the mouth as she rocked back and forth on his cock.

"Do you know how difficult it's been not to touch you the last five days?" he muttered into her ear. "I've missed your little pussy, sweetheart. Have you missed my cock?"

"Yes," she panted. "Yes, Caleb."

"Good." He licked a searing path across her collarbone. "I'm not going to last long, not with the way your tight pussy is squeezing my cock."

She moaned again, and her entire body shuddered when Caleb worked his hand under her skirt and rubbed at her clit. She ground to a halt, her back arching as he tugged at her clit before rubbing it again with his rough thumb.

"Oh, oh, oh…" she shouted. "Oh God, Caleb! I can't, I'm…"

"That's right, sweetheart," he said. "Don't hold back. I want to feel you coming all over my cock."

His hot breath and demands pushed her over the edge, and she screamed as her orgasm rushed through her. She squeezed him tightly, barely hearing his loud groan as she buried her face in his neck and panted.

When she had caught her breath, he gripped the back of her neck and pulled her into a sitting position. "My turn, sweetheart. Lift your skirt so I can see your pussy take all of my cock."

Her face flushing, she bunched her skirt around her waist again, holding it up as Caleb gripped her hip with one hand and kept the other around the back of her neck. He thrust back and forth, his low groans growing progressively louder as he watched his cock slide in and out of her.

"You feel so good, sweet Ellie," he moaned. "So wet and tight."

She knew he was close to coming and tried to squirm off his lap. She would finish him with her hand or mouth. She couldn't allow him to come inside her anymore. They were lucky she hadn't gotten pregnant before. She couldn't expect that luck to last.

"Where are you going?" he growled as his hand tightened on her hip.

"You – you can't come in me," she gasped out as he thrust hard into her wet pussy. "I'll finish you with my mouth."

"Like hell, you will," he said in a low groan. "This is my pussy, remember? If I want to come in it, I will."

"You can't!" she gasped as he thrust harder.

He pulled her head down and kissed her hard on the mouth. "I can and I will. Besides," he reached under her skirt and stroked her clit roughly, "I think you want me to come in you."

"You shouldn't," she gasped as new flames of desire licked at her veins. Why did the thought of being pregnant with Caleb's baby turn her on so much? She rubbed her pussy frantically against his fingers as he gave her a hard grin.

"You really want me to pull out right now, sweetheart?"

"No!" she cried, then pressed her lips together as he laughed softly.

"What do you want?"

"Caleb, please."

"Tell me." He pinched her clit hard and held it with his fingers as he fucked her roughly. "Tell me, my sweet."

"I need to come," she moaned as he tugged on her clit. It nearly sent her over the edge, and she moaned in dismay when he stopped immediately.

"I know what you need," he said. "Tell me what you want, and I'll let you come."

"I want you to come in me!" she shouted.

"That's my good girl," he whispered into her ear before releasing her clit. He rubbed it lightly with the tips of his fingers, and she screamed again as her second orgasm roared through her. It was more intense than the first one, and she shook wildly as pleasure shot through her veins. Dimly, she was aware of Caleb's hoarse shout of pleasure, of the way his hands dug into her hips as he thrust a final time and warmth flooded through her. He pressed her head against his chest and held her tight, not allowing her to move at all until his cock had softened completely. When he finally let her slide from his lap, she collapsed weakly on the sofa and watched as he buttoned his pants.

He leaned down and kissed her sweetly before rearranging her torn chemise and buttoning her shirt. He smoothed her skirt and kissed her again.

"I'll start the chores while you start dinner."

"I – all right," she whispered.

He squeezed her breast affectionately before standing and putting on his boots and jacket. "I won't be long," he said as he whistled for Scout and opened the door.

She nodded but stayed where she was as he and the dog left for the barn.

CHAPTER 11

"Caleb, I must speak with you about something important," Ellie said in a low voice.

He sat back in the chair as Ellie cleared the table and set the dishes in the sink. He prepared himself mentally for her anger. He was surprised it had taken her this long to unleash on him about earlier. He had deliberately ignored her request not to come inside of her and had withheld her orgasm until she said what he wanted to hear. It made him a bastard, but to his surprise, he didn't feel bad about it. The way her pussy had squeezed him when he refused to pull out, the extra surge of wetness that had coated his cock had convinced him she wanted him to come inside of her.

Once he was outside doing the chores and away from her sweet scent and delectable body, common sense had returned. While he still didn't feel much shame for what he had done, he had no doubt that she would be furious with him when he returned to the house. To his surprise, she was quiet but didn't seem angry. They'd eaten supper, and she'd even asked him more questions about his childhood.

"Caleb?" Ellie said.

He tried to smile charmingly at her. "Of course, Ellie. Go ahead."

She cleared her throat and gave him an oddly nervous look. "You know that I appreciate all that you have done for me. Allowing me to stay with you in exchange for cleaning and cooking has been a great help to me."

"I'm happy to help you," he said as she picked at the top of the table with her fingernail.

"The thing is," she took a deep breath, "I need money. Now that my relationship with my father is fractured, I want to return East."

"Go back East?" he repeated dumbly. He felt like he'd been punched in the stomach.

"Yes," she said. "I have an aunt there – my mother's younger sister. She would take me in."

He stared silently at her, and she said hurriedly, "But I require money to travel to my aunt's home."

"Ellie, I wish I could pay you for the cleaning, but I - "

"I know," she said. "I don't expect you to pay me wages. But I think it's time that I returned to town and found employment elsewhere."

"There is no employment to be found in town," he said.

Ellie's gaze flickered to the saloon dress. It was still lying on the chest in the living area, and anger surged through him.

"No," he said.

"It is the only way to make money," she said.

"I said no, Ellie." He glared at her, and she crossed her arms across her chest, giving him a defiant look.

"You have no right to tell me what to do. I am not your wife."

"You're not working there."

"I am."

His nostrils flared, and she gasped when he shoved his

chair back and stood. He stalked to the dress and gathered it up as she followed him.

"Caleb, what are you doing? What – no, stop that!"

He ignored her hands tugging at his arm, and threw the dress into the fire. The flames licked at the cloth, and she slugged him on the arm before letting loose with a string of curses that would have made a sailor blush.

Finally, panting loudly and glaring at him, she said, "It doesn't matter. Millie will have another dress that I can wear."

"You are not going back to the saloon," he said.

"What are you going to do? Keep me prisoner here? Will you tie me to the bed while you do the chores?"

He made a low growl before moving toward her. She made a squeak of surprise and tried to back away, but he wrapped his arm around her waist and pulled her against him before pressing a gentle kiss against her mouth.

"I can tie you to my bed, sweetheart, but I won't leave you to do the chores. I can think of much more pleasant things to do to you."

He let his gaze linger on her breasts, and she blushed furiously before poking him in the back. "You cannot distract me with sex."

"I'm not trying to distract you," he said. "You're not returning to work at the saloon, end of discussion."

"It is not!" she snapped. "Just because I – I fuck you, doesn't mean you have the right to tell me what to do. I need money, and if that means I have to lie on my back and let a man have his way with me, then so be it!"

"No one touches you but me," he said quietly.

She snorted angrily at him. "It's my body and my decision to make. Not yours."

"And if you're pregnant with my child?" he asked.

Her mouth dropped open, and she blinked at him. "I am not carrying your child."

"You don't know that," he said.

"I just had my cycle," she said. "You know I am not pregnant."

"We just had sex."

"I – we..." She trailed off, and he cupped her face and stroked her cheek.

"We had sex, Ellie. You could be carrying my child, and until we know for certain, you're not going anywhere. For the next month, you remain here in my home."

She stared blankly at him. He had a feeling she was still processing what he'd said, and he scooped her up and carried her into the bedroom. He undressed her quickly before tucking her under the covers and stripping off his clothes. He climbed into the bed beside her and pulled her into his arms.

"I don't want to have sex," she said in a low voice.

His chest tightened painfully, but he made himself smile at her. He had basically told her she was a prisoner in his home for the next month. Of course she would no longer want him.

"I just want to keep you warm, my sweet," he said. He rubbed Ellie's back and tucked her face into his neck. She lay stiffly against him at first, but it didn't take long for her body to relax against his. He made soft noises of comfort as he rubbed her back but was still surprised when she fell asleep. He eased back, and she whined, a frown wrinkling her forehead. She threw her arms around him and burrowed her body against his.

Her dark hair was still braided, and he stroked the braid lightly and pressed kisses against her bare shoulder. What a fine mess he had made of this. He loved Ellie, and she wanted to leave him. His only chance was to –

Love?

His entire body stiffened. He loved Ellie. Guilt immediately flooded through him.

I'm sorry, Missy.

There was only silence in his head, and he realized with a start that he couldn't remember the last time he heard Missy's voice in his head. He had spent every day of the previous two years having conversations in his head with his dead wife and hadn't even noticed that she had finally fallen silent.

More guilt ate at his stomach and he swallowed heavily.

I'm sorry, Missy, but I love her. I want to spend the rest of my life with her. I promise I'm not forgetting you, but I can't live without her. She's different from you but that's probably a good thing, right? She -

My darling, stop.

Missy's soft voice put a stop to his jumbled thoughts.

I'm sorry.

Don't be sorry, my darling. I want you to be happy. Ask her to marry you, give her babies, and live a good life.

She won't marry me. Not after the way I used her. Her father disowned her because of me. She'll never believe that I love her.

Missy didn't reply, and he sighed loudly. His only chance was if she were to get pregnant with his child. If she carried his child, she would have to marry him. He would spend the rest of his life showing her that he loved her and was sorry for what he had done to her.

His inner voice immediately spoke loudly and vehemently. *She won't be pregnant after one bout of lovemaking. You need to sleep with her every day. You need to –*

He cut off his inner voice. Ellie wouldn't sleep with him again after what he said to her tonight.

Seduce her.

A wave of bitterness went through him. He would not do

that to her again. If she came to him over the next month, he would not turn her away, but he wouldn't deliberately seduce her.

He didn't realize he was squeezing her tightly until she made a small sound of discomfort and raised her head to blink blearily at him.

"Too tight," she whimpered.

"I'm sorry, my love," he said. He loosened his hold, and she pressed her mouth against his before giving him a sleepy smile.

"Good night, Caleb."

"Good night, sweetheart."

She rested her head on his chest, and he rubbed her back as he stared into the darkness.

* * *

HE WOKE TO THE FEEL OF HER SOFT HAIR BRUSHING AGAINST his thighs. She had unbraided it, and his breath caught in his throat when she leaned over him and took his cock into her mouth. The sun was rising, and he studied how her dark hair gleamed in the light before reaching down and threading his fingers through the dark strands. He held tightly as she sucked slowly and firmly before tracing her tongue around the sensitive head.

"Ellie," he moaned as she stroked him with her hand before sucking on just the head.

She released him with a soft pop and smiled up at him. "Good morning, Caleb."

He moaned again when she licked his cock before sliding nearly all of him into her mouth. He groaned and tightened his hold on her head, thrusting his hips back and forth as she sucked enthusiastically.

When she pulled away, he made a sound of frustration

that ended the moment she straddled him. She rubbed her wet pussy against his cock before sliding him deep into her warmth. He gripped her hips, staring at her full breasts as she rode him slowly. Her back arched, and she made a low moan of need.

"Touch me," she whispered.

He rubbed her clit, teasing the swollen nub with his fingers until she made a harsh cry and her pussy tightened around him. She shuddered with pleasure before leaning forward and bracing her hands on his chest.

She rode him hard and fast, watching his face as he cupped her ass and squeezed it tightly. He had no idea why she was fucking him again, but he wasn't about to stop her. He was growing close already, and a trickle of guilt threaded through him. He wanted to come in her. He desperately wanted to increase the possibility of getting her pregnant, but the lack of shame over his behaviour last night had changed. He couldn't do that to her again – forcing her to be with him when she wanted to leave wasn't fair.

"I'm close," he whispered harshly.

Her hips slowed, and she stared silently at him. There was a look on her face that he didn't quite understand, and he made a hoarse moan of pleasure when she abruptly began to ride him hard.

"Ellie," he rasped as his hands dug into her hips, "did you hear me? I'm going to come."

She rode him faster in response, her ass slapping against his thighs as she cupped her breasts and tugged on her nipples.

"Sweetheart," he moaned as he watched her slender fingers play with her nipples, "stop for a minute. Use your mouth to... oh God!"

Ellie's tight pussy had grown even tighter as she clenched her muscles around him. He made another hoarse shout of pleasure as his orgasm surged through him. He was helpless to stop as Ellie's pussy squeezed and released him. His fingers bit into her hips, and he drove his pelvis upward and came deep inside of her. Shuddering wildly, he thrust back and forth as his seed filled her. He collapsed against the bed with a harsh moan. Ellie was still straddling him with that odd look on her face.

"I'm sorry," he said. "I swear I didn't mean to - "

She leaned down and cut his words off with a kiss. He stared blankly at her when she straightened and rubbed his chest before climbing off of him. "I'm going to get cleaned up and then start breakfast."

"Ellie - "

"You should start the chores. It's late." She put on her chemise and left the bedroom.

* * *

ELLIE EASED OUT OF THE BED. CALEB WAS STILL SLEEPING EVEN though it was past dawn. She dressed quietly and felt his forehead. It was cool to the touch, and she tucked the covers firmly around him before slipping out of the bedroom. He hadn't felt well yesterday, and when they'd gone to bed, his cheeks were red, and he'd had an obvious fever. It appeared the fever had broken in the night, but she decided to do the chores and allow Caleb to sleep. He had looked so tired and worn out last night.

Maybe it's because you keep having sex with him every chance you get.

She blushed a little as she built up the fire in the wood stove. It was true. It was three days since Caleb told her she wasn't allowed to leave his home until they knew she wasn't pregnant. She'd spent most of it seducing him into having sex with her.

Shame filled her, but she ignored it grimly. She had seen the look on Caleb's face when he talked about her being pregnant. She wasn't stupid. He wanted her to be pregnant. The man obviously wanted a child, and now that she knew he wouldn't abandon her or the baby, she had formulated a new plan.

Despite what she told him, she had no desire to leave this place and live with her aunt. Even if she could return East without becoming a whore at the saloon, she didn't want to go. She loved Caleb and wanted to spend the rest of her life with him. She knew that with certainty. Caleb didn't love her and would never marry her, but he wanted a baby. He would allow her to live with him permanently if she carried his child.

You don't know that for certain, Ellie, her inner voice said worriedly. *What if you have his child, and then he forces you to give up the baby to him and leave his home? What if he finds another woman to marry and lets her raise your child? What then? Not only will you not have Caleb, but you won't have your baby either.*

That won't happen, she thought grimly. If she did get pregnant, she would show Caleb over the next few months that she was strong enough to be a farmer's wife. It was doubtful he would marry her even if she didn't show weakness around him, but Caleb was a good and honourable man and would never take her child from her.

Is he? He used you to get revenge for his dead wife and child.

She ignored her inner voice. Caleb may have used her, but she also used him - neither of them was innocent. She headed to the door and pulled on her boots before reaching for her jacket.

Caleb was confused by her actions the last few days, but he hadn't turned her away once. The first few times they made love, he warned her when he was going to come, but when she continued to ignore him, he stopped telling her. He had tried multiple times to apologize for his behaviour the night he told her she couldn't leave, but she had quickly changed the subject each time or seduced him into taking her to his bed instead.

So, you're going to avoid the topic by distracting him with sex every time he brings it up?

Yes, that was exactly what she would do. She had limited time to get pregnant, and if that meant having sex with Caleb several times a day, she would do it. She loved him, and if carrying his child was the only way to stay with him, so be it.

She buttoned her jacket and patted Scout, who was hovering at her feet. "C'mon, boy," she said in a low voice. "I'm going to do the chores this morning. Caleb needs rest, and it'll show him that I'm not as fragile as he thinks. Right?"

The dog panted happily, and she petted his silky ears before opening the door. The cold air washed over her, and she bent her head against the wind before closing the door and hurrying forward. She stumbled and nearly fell when she walked into Scout. The dog stood as still as a statue, and she slapped him lightly on the rump.

"Scout, move."

A low, rumbling growl rose from his chest, and his hackles rose. Her pulse sped up in response, and she touched Scout's back tentatively. "What's wrong?"

"Hello, Ellie."

Her head whipped up, and she stumbled back. She stared at the man standing by the corner of the house.

"Father?" she whispered. "Wh-what are you doing here?"

"I've missed you," he said. He stepped toward her, and Scout flattened his ears and growled loudly. Her father gave the dog a nervous look, and Ellie patted Scout's flank before opening the door.

"Enough, Scout. It's all right. Go back in the house."

The dog whined but did what she asked. She shut the door before giving her father a guarded look. "How did you get here?"

"Carriage," he said. "It's out on the road behind the house. The driver is waiting for us."

"Us?" Ellie said.

"I'm here to take you home."

"So you can marry me off to Frederick?"

Her father shook his head. "No. *Home*, Ellie – back East."

"What?" Ellie gave him a look of shock. "You're leaving? Why?"

"Does it matter?" he said impatiently. "I'm here to get you so we can leave this wretched place and start over."

"Start over?" Ellie said. "You kicked me out, Father. I had nowhere to go, and now you want me to pretend that never happened?"

Her father winced. "I know, my darling child. I'm so sorry. I was a fool to abandon you the way I did. I have realized my error, and I'm here to make amends. I'm your father, Ellie. Pack your things and come with me. I can't stand the thought of leaving you behind in this wretched place."

"Leaving me behind? You threw me out of my home! Where was your compassion three weeks ago?" Ellie said angrily. "The cruelty you displayed to your own child is beyond – "

"Enough!" her father retorted. He glared at her, but she refused to apologize or cringe away like she would have in the past. "I am your father, and you will respect me."

"You stopped being my father the moment you abandoned me to my fate," Ellie said in a low voice.

He sighed again and arranged his face into a mask of forced patience. "My dear, I know what the farmer told you must have been difficult to stomach, but you must understand I had no choice. Those cowboys were going to kill me, and I had to borrow the money from Frederick. I was certain I could pay him back, and when I couldn't, I – I suppose I panicked. He was interested in you and agreed to forget the loan if I gave you to him."

Ellie stared wide-eyed at him, and he frowned at her. "Truthfully, this is your fault. If you hadn't allowed that filthy farmer to take your innocence, none of this would have happened. When Frederick found out you were no longer pure, he demanded that I repay him the loan. He only gave me a month to repay it, Ellie! I cannot meet the demands of his loan, so I'm leaving, and I want you to come with me. Now, grab your things quickly so we can leave. I have not told anyone we're leaving, and considering my current debt to Frederick, it's best if it remains that way."

"You – you tried to sell my virginity to Frederick," Ellie whispered.

There was a loud buzzing in her ears, and her hands shook wildly. She felt sick to her stomach, and she could barely hold back the bile that rose in her throat.

"The farmer didn't tell you," her father said as the door burst open and Caleb ran outside.

* * *

CALEB FROWNED AS ELLIE LICKED HIS FACE AGAIN.

"Sweetheart, don't do that," he muttered. She ignored him and licked his forehead. He grunted loudly and tried to push her away gently. He got a handful of fur, and his eyes popped open. Scout was standing over him on the bed, and Caleb made a sound of disgust when the dog licked his mouth.

"Scout, down. What are you doing in here?"

The dog jumped off the bed and whined loudly. Caleb sat up and rubbed his hands through his hair before glancing at

Ellie's side of the bed. It was empty, and he frowned at Scout. "Why did she let you in here?"

The dog whined again, and Caleb stretched before climbing out of bed and dressing slowly. He felt better today than yesterday, and the nausea in his stomach was gone. He even felt a thin thread of hunger as he buttoned his pants. He hoped Ellie was making pancakes for breakfast. God, he loved her pancakes. He stopped and suddenly sniffed the air. He couldn't smell any food cooking, and it sent unease through him. Where was Ellie? It was later than they normally slept, so why hadn't she started breakfast?

"Ellie? Ellie, where are you?" He called for her and when there was no answer, he pulled his shirt over his head and nearly ran out of the bedroom. There was no sign of her, and his heart sank. Had she run away?

Scout was whining and scratching at the door and he yanked his boots on and threw open the door. Scout shot past him, and he ran outside, stopping abruptly when he saw Ellie standing a few feet from the door. Her cheeks were bright red, and her body shook wildly.

He jogged over to her and put his arms around her. "Sweetheart, what are you doing out here? Come inside before you freeze to death."

She stared up at him, and his heart stuttered to a stop at the look of hurt in her eyes. "Ellie? What's wrong?"

She turned her head slowly, and he followed her gaze. Her father stood a few feet away, and Caleb pushed Ellie behind him. "Get off my land."

"I'm here for my daughter," Abraham said as Scout growled at him.

"Leave," Caleb said. He turned and grasped Ellie by the upper arms. "Sweetheart, go inside right now."

"You didn't tell me," she whispered.

"Tell you what?"

"You knew that father tried to sell my virginity to Frederick, and you – you didn't tell me."

"I'm sorry," Caleb said. "You were upset, and I didn't want to hurt you more."

"You should have told me," Ellie said.

"I know. I'm sorry."

"It's time to go, Ellie," her father said.

Caleb turned to face him. "What are you talking about?"

"I am returning East, and Ellie is coming with me."

"No, she isn't."

"She's my daughter," Abraham spat, "and she will do as I tell her."

"You abandoned her!" Caleb shouted. "You tried to sell her off to pay your debt, and when that didn't work, you abandoned her and left her to fend for herself with no thought of her safety or well-being."

"I have apologized to Ellie, and she has accepted my apology," Abraham said stiffly. "Not that it's any of your business. Come, Ellie. We cannot keep the driver waiting any longer."

"Ellie, you can't go with him," Caleb said desperately as Ellie stared blankly at her father. "Please, sweetheart."

He cupped her face and pressed a kiss against her mouth. "I love you. Please don't leave me."

Her eyes widened, and she bit at her bottom lip. "You - you love me?"

"Yes," he said. "I love you, I swear it."

"How sweet," Abraham said. "The poor farmer in love with the doctor's daughter. Ellie, do not listen to him. He may love you, but he cannot provide for you. We will return home and find you a husband who will not let you starve to death on the prairies. They don't need to know of your shameful past. No one does."

Ellie touched his cheek with a trembling hand, and Caleb pressed a kiss against her fingertips. She traced his jawline before taking a deep breath and turning to her father. "I'm not going with you, Father."

Abraham's mouth dropped open. "You are. Of course you are."

"No, I am not. I love Caleb, and I won't leave him," Ellie said.

"You cannot be in love with a farmer!" Abraham snapped. "Stop this foolishness at once and get in the carriage. I will not ask you again, nor will I - "

"I'm pregnant with his child," Ellie said calmly.

"You can't be," her father said

"I am."

"You whore!" Abraham screamed. "After everything I have done for you, all that I sacrificed to raise you after your mother died, you would humiliate me this way? You're nothing but a - "

His voice broke, and he screamed shrilly as Caleb stomped toward him. He punched Abraham in the face, knocking the man flat on his back into the deep snow. Blood pouring from his split lip, Abraham tried to scramble away as Caleb grabbed him and yanked him to his feet.

"Say one more word about her, and I'll kill you," he snarled at the terrified doctor.

"Caleb, stop."

Ellie's soft voice broke through his haze of anger. He released her father and stepped back as Ellie put her arm around his waist. Caleb pulled her close as she stared at her father.

"Your mother would be so disappointed in you," Abraham said bitterly as he spat blood into the snow.

"No," Ellie said quietly. "She would be disappointed in you, Father. How you have treated me would have broken her heart, and I am glad she isn't here to see it."

"You don't know - "

"Enough," Ellie said. Her father stared angrily at her as she sighed. "I will never understand your cruelty to me. But I want you to know that I will never think of you again after this moment. You, however, will think of me every day and regret your actions when you are old and dying alone."

She took Caleb's hand. He squeezed it firmly and pressed a kiss against her forehead. She smiled sweetly at him before facing her father again. "Goodbye, Father."

She tugged on Caleb's hand and started toward the house without another glance at her father. Caleb followed her but stopped in the doorway when she walked inside. He studied her father before whistling for Scout. The dog squeezed past him, and Caleb stepped inside and closed the door.

* * *

ELLIE PACED BACK AND FORTH AS CALEB SHUT THE DOOR. Faintly, she could hear the carriage pulling away, and relief flooded her. She would never see her father again, and no part of her was upset, not after what she learned today.

"Ellie?" Caleb said cautiously as she continued to pace. "I'm sorry for not telling you what your father did, but I truly did not want to upset you even more. Learning what your father tried to do would have only hurt you."

"I know," she said slowly. "I understand why you kept it to yourself. No one wants to learn that their father is a monster."

"He's not a monster," Caleb said. "He just - "

"He is," she interrupted. "We both know it."

He sighed, and she studied his face before moving to the kitchen. "Come sit down, Caleb. You still look unwell."

"I'm fine," he replied, following her into the kitchen. "Sit down, and I'll make you tea."

"No, I'll make the tea."

He tried to argue, and she gave him a fierce look of disapproval. He sat with a thump as she heated the water and added the leaves to the teapot. They stayed silent while she made the tea, and when it was steeping, she finally joined him at the table.

She wanted to take his hand, but she folded them in her lap instead, and he gave her a solemn look.

"Are you pregnant, Ellie?"

She laughed. "I have no idea. It's too soon to tell. You know that, Caleb."

"Why did you tell your father you were?"

She shrugged. "I figured it was the fastest way to make him leave."

"If you are pregnant, I - "

"Do you really love me?" she asked. "Or did you just say that to keep me here in case I am carrying your child?"

He blinked at her, and she jerked in surprise when he pushed back his chair and dropped to his knees in front of her. He took her hands and kissed both before staring up at her. "I love you, Ellie. I want to marry you."

"You said I was too fragile to be a farmer's wife," she said quietly.

"I was wrong."

"Yes, you were," she replied. "Why do you love me? I seduced you for my own gain when we first met, and my father killed your wife and baby. How could you possibly love me?"

"You're not responsible for your father's actions, and I have told you before – you did not seduce me. I seduced you to get back at your father. It's something I am deeply ashamed of and - "

"Can we agree that we both indulged in some," she paused, "inappropriate and shameful behaviour when we first met and put it in the past?"

He nodded as relief crossed his face. "Yes."

"Good." She smiled at him. "I should start breakfast and you need to do chores."

"Ellie, will you – that is, do you love me?" he asked hesitantly.

She gave him a look of surprise. "Of course I do."

"Do you? Or are you telling me what I want to hear because you think I'll kick you out if you don't?"

"Caleb," she leaned forward and cupped his face, "I have loved you since the moment you rescued me from the saloon."

She kissed him lightly, and he immediately deepened the kiss. She pulled away with a gasp and smiled at him. "I love you, Caleb. I will always love you."

"I love you too," he said before pulling her into his lap. She laughed and put her arms around his shoulders before kissing his thick neck. "I need to make your breakfast."

"I'm going to saddle the horses, and we're riding into town," he said.

"What? Why?"

"We'll stop at the church and have the preacher marry us today."

She laughed and pulled on a piece of his hair. "You need a haircut first. How about we get married next week."

He grinned before kissing her again. "I guess I can wait a few more days."

"Good. Now let me go so I can make breakfast."

He released her and jumped to his feet before pulling her up and nuzzling her soft throat. "If you make me pancakes, after breakfast I'll take you to bed and eat your sweet pussy."

She blushed before smiling at him. "You have yourself a deal, Mr. Thornwell."

EPILOGUE

"Are you all right?"

"I'm fine," Caleb snapped before giving Joseph an apologetic look. "I'm sorry, Joseph."

"That's fine," Joseph said. He clapped Caleb on the back. "She'll be good. She's young and strong, and the doctor got here in plenty of time. Don't worry. You'll hold your child in your arms before you know it."

"It's taking too long," Caleb said as he glanced at the closed bedroom door. "It shouldn't take this long for - "

He broke off as Ellie made a loud cry of pain. His face paled, and he sprinted for the door as the shrieking wail of a baby drifted through the door. Before he could open the door, Joseph was standing with him and pulling him back.

"Give them a minute," he said as Caleb tried to pull away.

"I need to see Ellie!" he snapped.

"You'll see her in a few minutes," Joseph said. "If there were a problem, the doctor would call for you."

Caleb paced for another ten minutes. Scout trailed after him, making small whimpers and whines of anxiety. He tried to soothe the dog but failed miserably as Joseph gave him a sympathetic look. He was about to storm into the bedroom when the door opened, and Louise appeared. In her arms was a small bundle of white fabric and Caleb watched in wonderment as a tiny hand appeared out of the fabric and flailed madly before there was an indignant wail of outrage.

"Would you like to meet your son, Caleb?"

"A son? I have a son," Caleb said.

Joseph hugged him roughly. "Congratulations, Caleb."

Louise placed the baby in Caleb's arms before moving to Joseph. He hugged her tightly as she gave him a quick kiss. "I'm going to stay the night in case Ellie needs me, but you should go home. Can you pick me up in the morning?"

He frowned at her. "We have not spent a night apart since we were married. I will go home and do the chores and then return to spend the night. If that's all right with you, Caleb?"

"Fine," Caleb said absently. He had barely heard Louise and Joseph's conversation. He studied his son's features, the red and wrinkled face, the dark hair that covered his skull, and the dent in his tiny chin. The baby made a small cry, and he swayed back and forth. "Hush, baby. Hush."

"He looks like you," Joseph said, peering over Caleb's shoulder.

Louise laughed. "He's the spitting image of his father."

"Ellie," Caleb said suddenly. "Is she all right?"

"She is," Louise said," You can see her in a while, but she asked me to bring the baby out to you."

Caleb gave her a grateful smile before kissing the baby's forehead. The baby began to wail, and Louise held out her arms. "Here, I'll return him to his mama."

She took the baby and Caleb sank into the sofa with a sigh of relief as Joseph grinned at him. "How's it feel to be a father?"

"Fine," Caleb muttered.

"Just fine?" Joseph said.

"I am worried about Ellie," Caleb said. He stared at the closed bedroom door before standing and pacing again.

"You heard Louise, she's fine. Come outside with me for a bit."

"I won't leave her," Caleb said.

"We'll be right outside. Louise will call for us if she needs us."

Sighing deeply and with a final look at the bedroom door, Caleb followed Joseph outside.

* * *

"I can't wait any longer," Caleb said to Joseph. It was two hours later, and he didn't care what Louise said earlier. He needed to see Ellie and confirm that she was all right. As he reached for the bedroom door, it opened, and the doctor and Louise stepped out. Louise was carrying bedding in her arms, and she brought it outside to the washtub.

"How is she?" Caleb asked the doctor anxiously.

"She's perfectly fine." The doctor smiled at Caleb. "Your wife did very well. She's tired and will need lots of rest for the next few days, but there weren't any complications. She's asking for you."

"Thank you," Caleb said hoarsely as Louise returned to the house. "Thank you so much."

"You're welcome," the doctor replied cheerfully. "Now, Mrs. Billings, do you think I could trouble you to tell me where the teapot is? I'd love a bit of tea before I head back to town."

"I'll make it for you," Louise said. "Come into the kitchen."

Joseph and the doctor followed her to the kitchen as

Caleb entered the bedroom. Ellie was lying on her side in the bed, staring sleepily at the baby in the cradle next to the bed. He carefully curled up behind her and pressed a kiss against her neck. "Hello, my love."

"Hello, Caleb." She smiled tiredly at him.

"How do you feel?" he asked.

"Very tired and sore," she said.

"I'm sorry."

"I'm not," she said before taking his hand and linking their fingers. "He's as handsome as his daddy."

"Are you sure you're all right?" he said.

She squeezed his hand. "Yes. Do not worry about me."

"Did he eat?" Caleb asked.

Ellie nodded before yawning. "Yes. The doctor said he latched on very well for his first time."

"You should get some sleep," he said before kissing her neck again.

"Hmm," she replied as her eyelids drifted closed. He stared at their son as Ellie's breathing slowed and deepened. She suddenly twitched against him and opened her eyes. "We need to decide on a name for him."

"We do," he said.

"I think we should name him after your father."

"Are you sure?"

She nodded. "Yes. I like the name Elliott, and I'm sure it will make your father happy to have a grandson named after him."

"It would," he said hoarsely. He kissed the top of Ellie's head as she studied their son.

"Hello, Elliott," she whispered. "I'm so happy to finally meet you, sweet boy."

Caleb kissed her again. "I love you, Ellie."

"I love you too, Caleb."

* * *

Keep reading for an excerpt from Elizabeth Kelly's small town romance, "Sweet Harmony".

SWEET HARMONY EXCERPT

COPYRIGHT © 2019 ELIZABETH KELLY

When the doorbell rang, Kira smoothed down her blonde hair and checked her reflection in the toaster. Not that it mattered what she looked like. This wasn't a first date, for God's sake.

She headed out of the kitchen and down the hallway. Two long windows flanked the front door, and she could see one tanned arm and hand through the right one. Her dentist had big hands.

You know what they say about big hands.

She flushed and tossed that errant thought out of her head before opening the door. She smiled at the dark-haired man standing on her front porch.

"Hello, Dr. MacMillan."

"Hello, Ms. Walker," he said.

There was a moment of awkward silence, and then she stepped back. "Call me Kira. Please, come in."

He stepped into the house, and she shut the door before squeezing past him. "Would you like something to drink? I have water, iced tea and soda. Or I can make coffee."

"An iced tea would be fine," he said.

As he followed her toward the kitchen, she wondered if he was checking out her ass in her yoga pants. She knew she didn't have a great body. She was on the thin side, and she secretly coveted Grace's full curves. She scoffed inwardly. Who was she kidding? Forget Grace's curves, she'd take Addison's very respectable C-cup boobs if given the chance. She was barely a B-cup, and her cleavage was thanks to the miracle invention of the century – the push-up bra.

Why she even thought her dentist would check out her ass was ridiculous. It was flat and –

Hey, Kira? Maybe you should stop thinking about your own damn tits and ass and get the man his iced tea.

Dr. MacMillan was hovering in the kitchen doorway while she stood blankly next to the fridge, and she gave him an embarrassed smile. "Sorry. Have a seat, and I'll get that iced tea."

"Thank you," he said.

She poured each of them a glass of iced tea and perched on the edge of the chair across from him. He drank some iced tea before saying, "It's good. Thanks."

"I like it a little on the sweet side," she said. "My brother says it's way too sweet and that I'll rot my teeth right out of my head, but I guess that's why I go to see you, right? To keep my teeth from rotting out of my head when I eat too much sweet stuff?"

Kira! Enough!

She shut her mouth with a snap. Fuck, what was wrong with her? Why was she so damn nervous? Sure, Dr. MacMillan was handsome enough, but he wasn't Daniel. She closed her eyes for a moment and conjured up an image of Daniel. It calmed her a little, and she took a deep breath. Daniel's blond hair and dark blue eyes were what she wanted.

Dr. MacMillan's eyes might be blue, but they were so

light they were almost transparent. She could see none of the warmth and humour in them that Daniel's gaze had. In fact, her dentist was currently staring at her like she was some new and interesting species of bug he had discovered crawling up his leg.

She cleared her throat. "Sorry, I babble when I'm nervous."

He took another drink of iced tea. "You have a nice home."

"Thank you. It was my childhood home. It belongs to my brother now, but he didn't want to live here. My parents died a few years ago, and being in the house brought on too many sad memories for him. I love living here, though. It makes me feel closer to my mom and dad, you know?"

She closed her mouth again. Holy shit, she was making the worst first impression ever.

"I'm sorry about your parents." His voice was a low rasp, and the sound of it sent the weirdest shiver down her spine.

"Thank you," she replied. "So, um, Grace said we could help each other with our problems."

He nodded. "Possibly."

She waited and tried not to sigh with frustration when he said nothing else. His silence was beginning to unnerve her. Daniel was chatty and always the life of the party. She could barely get a word in edgewise when she was with him, and she loved that. She loved his bold brashness and how he lit up a room when he walked into it.

Her dentist hardly made an impact. Hell, she'd met him how many times in his office, and she had no impression of him at all. He was just a masked guy who came in and checked her teeth at the end of the cleaning.

"So, you need a date for your cousin's wedding?" she asked.

"Yes," he said, "and you need a boyfriend to make Daniel Moore jealous."

His voice had the slightest hint of derision, and she immediately blushed. It was evident that he thought she was an idiot.

"You know what? Never mind, Dr. MacMillan." She stood and dumped her iced tea down the sink. "This isn't going to work. I'll show you out now."

She stalked toward the front door. She could hear him behind her, but before she could open the door, he wrapped his long fingers around her wrist. The touch of his skin against hers made another one of those little shivers zip down her spinal cord. She froze and turned to stare up at him.

"I'm sorry," he said. "I'm being an ass."

"Yes, you are."

He sighed and dropped her wrist before raking his hand through his dark hair. "I apologize. Also, if we're going to fake date, you should call me Connor."

"Why are you even here, Connor?" she asked. "It's obvious you think this is a stupid idea."

"It isn't," he said. "I'm just -"

He paused and rubbed at one temple. "What if this doesn't work?"

"What do you mean?"

"What if our fake dating doesn't make Daniel jealous? Will you still go with me to my cousin's wedding? Still pretend to be my girlfriend?"

"Yes," she said.

"What if it does work? Then what? You start dating Daniel, and I'm headed to Willington alone."

"Well, your cousin's wedding is in a month, right?"

"Yes."

"We don't have to start fake dating right away. We can

give it a couple of weeks and use that time to learn more about each other. It's probably a good idea if we know more than each other's names. It'll be more believable if we know personal stuff about each other. That leaves only two weeks until your cousin's wedding. I think it'll take more than a couple of weeks to make Daniel jealous," she said.

"Do I have your word that you'll attend the wedding with me?" he asked.

"Yes," she said. "I'll be there, no matter what."

Then we have an agreement," Connor said. "You'll pose as my girlfriend at my cousin's wedding, and I'll help you make Daniel seethe with jealousy and realize that you're his soul mate."

She gave him a dirty look. "You don't have to make it sound so juvenile."

He just shrugged, and she reached for the front door. "Thank you. I'll get your number from Grace and text you in the next few days about meeting to go over personal stuff."

"There's just one more thing," Connor said.

"What?"

"This." He gripped the back of her neck and pulled her forward. She made a decidedly stupid-sounding squeak when he bent his dark head and pressed his mouth against hers. She stood stock-still with her eyes wide and unblinking as he slid his other arm around her waist and pulled her against his hard body.

When he sucked on her lower lip, a strange tingle went through her lower body, and another small sound escaped her lips. This one, embarrassingly enough, sounded like a moan, and she tried to step back. His hand tightened around her neck, holding her completely immobile. When his tongue slid across her upper lip, she heard another of those odd moan-like noises as her eyes drifted shut.

God, he smells so good, she thought bewilderedly as he

tilted her head back. He kissed her again, his lips warm and weirdly persuasive, and it took her a minute to realize she was returning his kiss.

Kira! Stop kissing your dentist!

It was solid advice, but her body was completely and blissfully betraying her. She pressed up against Connor and put her arms around his neck. He was so tall that it was a real stretch to do it, but she liked the way it forced her breasts against his chest.

His tongue licked the seam of her mouth. Her head whirling and her pussy suddenly throbbing, she parted her lips. He slid his tongue between them and tasted her with slow, long licks that made Kira shudder with pleasure. He tasted sweet, like the iced tea he had been drinking. When she pushed her tongue into his mouth with a decided lack of finesse, he slid his fingers into her hair and tugged her back.

"Slow," he whispered.

She blushed fiercely. For roughly a nanosecond, she thought about telling him to stop, but then his warm mouth returned to hers, and he was urging her tongue back into his mouth with slow licks of his. She slowed down and mimicked the slow strokes of his tongue.

He groaned quietly. Besides his low whisper, it was the first sound he had made since kissing her. It flamed the lust in her belly even higher. She had a feeling that the icy Dr. Connor MacMillan never lost control. The idea that kissing her could make that control slip, even a little, was deliciously intoxicating.

She arched her back and rubbed her abdomen against the hardness pressing into it. Connor was hard. He was hard for her, and that sent another flickering flame of excitement through her nerve endings. She rubbed her small breasts against him and wondered what she could do to get him to touch them. Her nipples were almost painfully hard and poking against her bra. A sudden vision of Connor sucking on them brought on a gush of liquid that soaked the crotch of her panties.

He pulled away abruptly, and she would have fallen in a boneless heap to the floor if he hadn't steadied her. She stared dumbly at him before reaching up and touching her trembling, swollen lips.

"Why-why did you do that?" she whispered.

"If we're posing as boyfriend and girlfriend, it's going to require physical touching and kissing," he said.

She felt like she'd been through the wringer, but he wasn't even out of breath. If it hadn't been for the way his dick still strained at the front of his pants, she would have thought he was completely unaffected by the kiss between them.

"O-only when we're around other people." She couldn't seem to stop stuttering or touching her swollen mouth.

He gave her an impatient look. "It won't look very realistic if we kiss each other like it's the first time we've ever kissed. And I wanted to see if we had chemistry."

"Do we?" she asked like an idiot.

A brief smile crossed his face, sending a weird tingle down the base of her spine. "Yes. I think so, anyway."

She didn't reply, and he patted her shoulder like he was his sister. "That's a good thing, Kira. It will make it appear more real."

"Uh, right," she said.

He studied her. "How many men have you kissed before?"

"Why?"

"You're not," he paused, "great at kissing."

Her face was so red she was nearly sweating, and she gave him a furious look. "That's a really rude thing to say."

"No, just honest. We'll need to practice some more."

She wanted to tell him to take his idea of practice kissing and stuff it up his piehole, but strangely the thought of kissing him again wasn't entirely unpleasant. Besides, as much as it was a blow to her ego, he probably had a point. She'd kissed two men before him, and neither of them had provoked the type of reaction that her dentist's kiss did.

He opened the front door and asked, "What time do you work tomorrow?"

"Uh, I need to be at the office by nine."

"I'll stop by at eight, and we'll practice." He left, shutting the door quietly behind him, and she sank against the wall, her fingers still tracing her lower lip. What the hell just happened?

ABOUT THE AUTHOR

Elizabeth Kelly was born and raised in Ontario, Canada. She moved west as a teenager and now lives in Alberta with her husband and a menagerie of pets. She firmly believes that a person can survive solely on sushi and coffee, and only her husband's mad cooking skills prevents her from proving that theory.

For more information about Elizabeth, check out her website at

www.elizabethkelly.ca

facebook.com/EKellyBooks

x.com/ElizabethKBooks

instagram.com/elizabethkelly_author

amazon.com/Elizabeth-Kelly/e/B00EOHZ0MS

bookbub.com/authors/elizabeth-kelly

ALSO BY ELIZABETH KELLY

Tempted Series

Tempted

Twice Tempted

Forever Tempted

Breathless

Tempted Trilogy (Books 1-3)

Red Moon Series

Red Moon

Red Moon Rising

Dark Moon

Alpha Moon

Pale Moon

The Recruit Series

The Recruit (Book One)

The Recruit (Book Two)

The Recruit (Book Three)

The Recruit (Book Four)

The Recruit (Book Five)

The Recruit (Book Six)

The Shifters Series

Willow and the Wolf (Book One)

Ava and the Bear (Book Two)

Place Your Trust in Me (Book Three)

Individual Books

The Necessary Engagement

Amelia's Touch

The Rancher's Daughter

Healing Gabriel

The Contract

A Home for Lily

Saving Charlotte

Shameless

The Fairy Tales Collection

Broken

An Unlikely Seduction

Holiday Romance

The Christmas Wife

The Christmas Rescue

The Christmas Nanny

The Christmas Boss

Sordid Games